PIECES

MADDY REYNOLDS IN THE CROSSHAIRS

JOHN NETTI

Black Rose Writing | Texas

ISBN: 978-1-68513-493-8
LIBRARY OF CONGRESS CONTROL NUMBER: 2024939365
PUBLISHED BY BLACK ROSE WRITING
www.blackrosewriting.com

Printed in the United States of America
Suggested Retail Price (SRP) $19.95

Pieces is printed in Minion Pro

*As a planet-friendly publisher, Black Rose Writing does its best to eliminate unnecessary waste to reduce paper usage and energy costs, while never compromising the reading experience. As a result, the final word count vs. page count may not meet common expectations.

PRAISE FOR
THE GLADES

John Netti's *The Glades* was selected as a winner of the 2023 PenCraft Seasonal Book Award Spring Competition. The PenCraft Seasonal Book Awards recognizes books of remarkable literary quality, artistic excellence, and popularity with readers. *The Glades* exemplified these criteria as a winner in the Fiction—Suspense genre.

I dedicate this book to the victims of violence who carry their emotional and physical scars with them each day.

Special thanks to Megan, Anne-Marie, and Fran, who helped make *PIECES* a more compelling story. Melissa, your proofreading was enormously helpful. To the beta readers, Denise, Jean-Marie, Pat, Nichole, Donna, Holly, Molly, John, Mike, Gary and Susan, your feedback and support were essential. Thank you to my wife, Jean, for putting up with my long absences while in the writing room and to David, Laura, Alexis, and Tyler, who are always being there for me. Finally, as always, thank you, God, for the gift of writing.

PIECES

Evil imaginations have no limits. Psalms 73:7

CHAPTER ONE

Maddy Reynolds
June 1996

Exhausted from driving three hours on the mountain roads, flashing lights ahead snapped her wide awake. New York State Police had set up a roadblock, and Maddy pulled up, lowering the window as a trooper walked to her Jeep.

"We don't mean to alarm you, ma'am, but we'd like to check your vehicle."

"Sure, go right ahead."

"Can I see your license, and can you please step out?"

She opened the door, got out, and handed him her license.

"Are you Maddy Reynolds, the detective?" he asked.

"Ex-detective. Can I ask what this is about?"

"We're looking for a stowaway." He handed her license back as two other troopers searched the Jeep.

She saw his name on his lapel tag. "What can you share with me, Trooper Lopez?"

"There's been a murder," he said.

"Can you tell me the name of the victim?" she asked.

"I'm not supposed to tell you this, but since you are law enforcement, the woman's name is Abigail Hicks."

Maddy's stomach sank. Abigail was a quiet, unlikely person to fall to such a fate.

"Do you live on the mountain across from the village?" Lopez asked.

"Yes, I do."

"You'll need to be very careful, Ms. Reynolds. There's a killer out there somewhere, and we think it was random."

Lopez let her pass, and when she entered the village, the trees along Main Street danced in the wind; a storm was coming. She pulled over near Lena's Diner and got out. Her hair blew back, a clattering Coke can toppled along the sidewalk, and an air of fevered excitement filled the diner as she entered.

The place echoed with loud chatter, and smoke from food frying in the kitchen hung in the air. The grease smell was like a Lenten Friday fish fry. *My God, this place is buzzing.* Rose, the server, and Maddy's dear friend, rushed to her.

"Did you hear what happened to Abigail?"

"Yes, they stopped me at a roadblock outside of town."

"Can you believe it?" Rose said. She stood with a pencil in one hand, an order pad in the other, and with her eyes bugging out as if she'd drunk a pot of high-test coffee. "Lester saw her in the post office this morning, and they found her body around noon at Blind Bluff. They think someone abducted her in her car, and she never made it home."

"Do they know who did it?" Maddy asked.

"A couple of troopers stopped in for lunch, and I overheard them using the name Whitfield."

Oh, Jesus. Maddy folded her arms, not wanting to alarm her friend, and said nothing.

"Why would anyone want to murder poor Abigail Hicks?" Rose said. "Ever since those people at The Glades killed her daughter, she had withdrawn into herself. She sure took Luellen's death awful hard, didn't she? The poor thing doesn't have any living family. And who the hell is this Whitfield guy, anyway? Do you know someone with that name in Berry Lake? I don't. My God, listen to me rambling on. I always talk like this when I'm scared." Maddy knew her friend's quirks, and it made her smile. "Shit, I have to take an order," Rose said. "I'll catch you later."

Maddy stared into her glass of ice water, thinking of Abigail's story. Her daughter was a victim of sex trafficking years earlier, and they found her body in the woods behind Maddy's home. Abigail was kind, and the idea of her suffering from Amos Whitfield bothered her deeply. Feeling a hand on her shoulder, she looked and saw Reverend Dietrich.

"Oh, hi, Reverend."

"Did you hear what happened?" he said as he sat on the stool beside her.

"Yes, Rose just told me."

"Berry Lake has seen more than its fair share of senseless violence, and now it's at our doorstep again," he said. "I'm afraid we're being tested." Noticing her exhaustion, he asked if she was okay.

"I just returned from Albany Medical, and I'm wiped out," she said. "I've been with Adam for the last week."

"Dear Lord, what happened to him?"

"He had brain surgery," Maddy said. The Reverend asked if he was alright.

"The surgery went well, and he's about to enter a rehab program for ten weeks."

"I've noticed he walks with a cane," Dietrich said. "Does he have multiple sclerosis?"

"No. Adam was an undercover detective with the New York State Police and received a gunshot wound to his head several years ago. He's been failing, and the corrective surgery is supposed to help."

"No wonder you look so tired," he said. "Is the surgery likely to succeed?"

"It's not clear. I'm concerned Adam's expectations are too high. He thinks he'll be able to walk without a cane when he finishes the program."

"Trust in God, Maddy. He'll give you and Adam what you need to get through this. I'll keep you two in my prayers," Dietrich said as he stood. He put his hand on her shoulder. "If you need to talk, I'm always available."

As he walked away, Maddy noticed an African American woman sitting in a booth and did a double take. It was Hannah Bates from the FBI. Maddy walked over and asked if she wanted company.

"Maddy Reynolds! Sure, have a seat."

"So, the killer is Amos Whitfield," Maddy said.

"What makes you say that?"

"They don't send in the big guns for a piddly murder."

Hannah smiled. "Yeah, we think so. We're setting up a command center in the elementary school."

"Why the hell would Whitfield come to Berry Lake?" Maddy said.

"Got me, but there's a reason. Everything Whitfield does has one. Did you know the victim?"

"Yes, I knew Abigail," Maddy said. "I take it the killer took a body part; otherwise, you wouldn't suspect Whitfield right away."

"I'm telling you this cop to cop," Hannah said. "He took her kidneys."

"Geez, why does he do that?"

"He only does it to women, and shrinks think it's because of his mother."

"Great," Maddy said. "We get blamed for everything."

"How well did you know the Hicks woman?" Hannah asked.

Rose came to the table to take their orders. When she left, Maddy answered.

"Abigail let me into her life during an excruciating time; she was grieving the loss of her daughter. She shared the details of Luellen's death with me, and it was about as close as she had let anyone get to her. After it happened, she stayed to herself and led a private existence."

"How did you know about Whitfield?" Hannah asked.

"People overhear lots of things in diners," Maddy said.

Hannah shook her head. "If it's him, I feel sorry for Berry Lake. The last time he was active was seven years ago, and he killed five people in six weeks. I think he's trying to catch up with Ted Bundy, and I'm keeping my fingers crossed he doesn't."

Rose brought out the food as Maddy sat with her arms crossed. Hannah picked up her sandwich to take a bite, but stopped.

"What is it, Maddy?"

"I was just thinking of what drives guys like Bundy and Whitfield."

"Don't forget Cupid," Hannah said.

"Yeah, Cupid, too. It's like they just can't stop killing."

"Cupid would have killed a lot more kids if you hadn't stopped him," Hannah said.

Maddy unfolded her arms, looked directly at the FBI agent, and asked, "Are you looking for a second body?"

Appearing startled, Hannah put her sandwich on the plate. "Who told you that?"

"No one told me. I researched Whitfield when I worked the Cupid case, and I remember he sometimes hides his victims in cars. Troopers stopped me at a roadblock outside of town. They claimed to be searching for a stowaway. No way were they looking for Whitfield. They must be looking for another body."

"Keep this confidential, Maddy."

"Of course," Maddy said as she sipped her water. Hannah started eating her sandwich, and Maddy asked who the second victim was.

"Abigail Hicks was raising a child, and she's missing."

"What? No one around here knows of Abigail raising a kid," Maddy said. "Are you sure?"

"As sure as can be. It looks as if Abigail tried keeping her from the world. The girl's bedroom was in the attic. Other than that, there was no sign a child lived there. Anyone visiting would never know it. We estimate the girl is about nine years old. There's no sign of her anywhere, and we are operating on the assumption that Whitfield killed her, too."

"The girl must be Luellen's child," Maddy said. "Abigail told me her daughter had come home from The Glades heartbroken over Avery Jordan. That was about nine years ago. She stayed home for several weeks before being killed when she returned. She must have had Jordan's baby before she left her mother. It's hard to believe Abigail raised the girl with no one knowing, but I suppose it's possible."

There was silence while Hannah ate. Maddy sipped her water, trying to understand Abigail's secret. *Rose said Lester saw her leaving the post office alone this morning, and they found her body at Blind Bluff around noon. Abigail must have known her killer and met him there. The woman has always been a loner, so she had to be living a double life. Strange,* she thought. Finally, Maddy asked Hannah how her family was.

"Anthony is Anthony; he's my rock," Hannah said. "When you're married to a psychiatrist, there's always someone there to tell you when you're going off the rails. Charles is doing well. He's just finished his first year at Albany University. How about you, Grandma?" Hannah said, chuckling.

"Don't rub it in," Maddy said. "Every time the twins call me that, I feel ancient. I never would have thought I'd be a grandmother at forty-four."

"How about Adam; how did the surgery go?" Hannah and Adam had worked together as detectives with the New York State Police.

"He's hoping it will restore his ability to walk, and only time will tell," Maddy said.

"Tell him I send my best." Hannah looked at her watch. "Oh dear, I have to get back to the command center." She put money on the table and hurried out.

Maddy watched FBI Agent in Charge Hannah Bates walking out of Berry Lake's only diner, feeling the gravity of what that meant.

When Maddy stepped outside, the sky was black, and a few large raindrops stung her face as she rushed to her Jeep. She got in, glanced at the empty passenger seat, and missed Adam.

Before she reached the road to her place, the rain was so heavy she could barely see ten feet in front of her vehicle. She grabbed her luggage bag and ran for the kitchen door when she got to her house. Drenched, she set the bag on the table, dripping water onto the tile floor.

Plopping into a kitchen chair, Maddy felt Adam's presence everywhere. She thought of the months he declined. She had spent nights encouraging him, sometimes without sleeping, and didn't want to admit that it was getting to her. *I have to get through this.*

The phone rang, and she answered.

"Hello?" She waited; there was silence.

"Who is this?" A click and a dial tone; the person hung up. The caller ID said *Private Number.*

The wind blew the curtains back, and she felt rain blowing in. She ran through the house, closing the windows, but the phone rang again, and a man's muffled voice spoke when she answered.

"Have you checked your mail?"

"Who the hell is this?" she shouted. He hung up again. Her heartbeat picked up as she ran to the bedroom, pulled the metal box from her closet shelf, and laid it on the bed. After rolling the numbers on the lock—1, 12, 13, 6—she lifted the top and grabbed one of her Glocks. She reached for a magazine, shoved it into the weapon, and ran to the kitchen, looking outside for movement.

A flash of light and a loud crack shook the house. Lightning had struck nearby, and the electricity was out when she tried a light switch. It was late afternoon, and the clouds were black. It was nearly dark. Her heart pounded. She was alone in her house on a mountain with no electricity and a deluge of rain, thunder, and lightning between herself and the village.

She stood hidden behind a curtain, looking out. Wanting to get to her mailbox, she moved the sliding kitchen door back, and a gust of wind and rain blasted her face. Lowering her head, she ran to the Jeep, opened the door, hopped inside, and lay the weapon on the passenger seat before starting the engine. The rain had soaked her. She shivered as she drove the gravel driveway and pulled over near the mailbox.

Lowering the window, she reached out and pulled the metal mailbox cover. She retrieved a box wrapped in a brown paper bag. Setting it on the seat next to the Glock, she started back up the road to her place and tucked the box and weapon under her arm to shield them from the rain as she ran into the house.

After placing the box and handgun on the counter, Maddy pulled out scissors and cut the paper and cardboard. A tightly wrapped plastic bag slid out, and a brown, rounded item the size of a fist floated in red liquid inside the bag.

"It's a fucking kidney!" she screamed. Holding her head, she stared at the grotesque human organ, and her stomach roiled. *It's Whitfield; he's coming after me.* Trying to catch her breath, she tucked the Glock into the back of her jeans running through the house, locking windows and doors. It felt like the night Cupid came to her home, taunting her before he tried to kill her.

She waited, keeping her eyes on the outside, looking for movement. An hour passed. Her heart slowed, and she collected her thoughts.

I need to talk with someone. Sidney Myers popped into her head. He was a criminal psychologist who specialized in serial killers. She shuffled through a desk drawer, found the address book, and called using her cell phone. He picked up on the fourth ring.

"Sidney, it's Maddy." She heard her voice quiver as she spoke.

"Maddy, what's wrong?" Holding her head in her hand, she sat at the kitchen table with the gun next to her. The room was nearly dark, and her body was wet and chilled.

"Amos Whitfield is in Berry Lake. He killed a local woman today and left one of her kidneys in my mailbox."

"Where are you right now?" Sidney said, alarmed.

"I'm at home alone, but I have a weapon," she said. "A storm has knocked out the electricity."

"Has the FBI set up a command center yet?"

"Yes, Hannah Bates is heading up the operation."

"You should call Bates. Whitfield is a very dangerous killer, Maddy. You're excellent with a handgun, but he's also supposed to be an expert. You probably haven't kept up your skills, and he probably has."

"I need to think about it," she said. She paused, then asked, "Why do you suppose he's doing this?"

"I know exactly why he's doing this," Sidney said. "He wants to take you down. The only plausible reason for Whitfield coming to Berry Lake is you."

"But why?"

"It's like the Old West. The fastest gun would become a target for other gunslingers to prove themselves. Everyone knows Maddy Reynolds killed Cupid, the child serial killer. You received a lot of publicity for taking down Avery Jordan at The Glades. Don't doubt it, Maddy; Amos Whitfield is in Berry Lake because of you." Exhaling a deep breath, Maddy felt the weight of Sidney's words.

"But why didn't he come after me directly?"

"What fun would that be? He can't impress you if you're dead. Whitfield is doing what he always does after moving into a town. But this time he has the renowned detective, Maddy Reynolds, watching him as a bonus. When he's ready, he will try to kill you; count on it." Sidney remained silent as if giving her a moment to digest what he was telling her before he continued.

"Whitfield is a psychopath and an extreme narcissist. He's gotten away with all those murders for so many years that he thinks he's untouchable. He feels godlike, smarter than law enforcement, and better than other people."

Maddy's mind was overwhelmed thinking of Abigail Hicks, the kidney, Hannah Bates—everything felt jumbled together.

"Maddy, are you there?"

"Yes, I'm here."

"What will you do?"

"I'm going to get out of these damn wet clothes. I'll hunker down and wait for the electricity to come back tonight.

"I meant, what will you do about telling the FBI what's happening?"

"I know what you meant, Sidney. I need to think about it."

"I'm here if you want to talk," he said.

It was pitch dark when she hung up. Rummaging through the kitchen drawer, she found a flashlight, three candles, and a box of matches. She lit the candles, spread them around the house, and changed her clothes.

She sat in the living room after drawing the curtains with her mind racing. *How can this be happening?*

The house was dark except for the flickering candlelight. The only sound was the wind swishing rain against the windows. Time passed, the candles grew shorter, and Maddy struggled to stay alert.

She heard a thud. *It's the outside basement door closing. Shit, I forgot to lock it.* Grabbing the flashlight and weapon, she stepped toward the kitchen basement door and turned the knob, shining the light at the stairs. A girl stood wide-eyed, looking up at her. *Could that be Abigail's granddaughter?*

Maddy held the weapon behind her and said, "I won't hurt you." The child looked at the outside door. "Don't run; I promise I won't hurt you." The girl was shivering. "I have dry clothes and food. My name is Maddy; what's yours?" The child didn't speak.

"I'll leave the flashlight on the top step and go to another room. You can take it and run away, but I hope you come inside; I'll be waiting." She placed the light on the stairs, went to the kitchen, and sat. She heard nothing; five minutes passed, then fifteen, and she thought the child had left. When she walked over to shut the basement door, the girl stood in the shadows, startling her. "I'm glad you came up," she said. "Would you like something to eat? The electricity is out, but I have milk and leftover pizza."

The child crept into the candlelight. Her red hair and freckled face shone. Her olive-black eyes were as mysterious as she. *My God, she's stunning.*

"Have a seat. I'll get the food." She went to the refrigerator, pulled out the pizza and milk, brought them to the table, and the girl started eating. Maddy watched with amazement.

"Is it good?" The girl nodded.

"Would you like ice cream?" Maddy asked when she finished. "I don't think it's melted yet."

"Yes, please," she said.

Returning with a bowl of chocolate ice cream, Maddy set it on the table before her. She slurped it into her mouth and Maddy said, "Not too fast; I don't want you to get sick." The child stopped eating, looked at her, and smiled.

"Will you tell me your name, please?" Maddy asked.

"I'm Phoebe," she said matter-of-factly before returning to her ice cream. The house shook, and the girl appeared startled.

"That's okay, Phoebe. It's only the electricity coming back on." She reassuringly put her hand on Phoebe's arm, and the girl continued eating. When she finished, Maddy brought the dish to the sink and turned, facing her.

"Would you like to stay here tonight? I have an extra bedroom, and it's nicer than sleeping in the woods."

"Can I take a bath?" Phoebe asked.

"Sure, you can. Come, let's change your wet dress.

Maddy turned on the bath water and took Phoebe to the dresser.

"Try this for a nightgown." She pulled out a long sweatshirt. "I think this should work; what do you think?" The girl smiled.

"I'll wash your clothes; they should be dry by morning," Maddy said. Phoebe undressed in the bathroom, and Maddy helped her into the tub.

"I'll wash your things and lock the basement door. I'll be right back."

Maddy's mind churned as she left Phoebe in the bathtub. *Adam is recovering from brain surgery; Amos Whitfield killed Abigail Hicks today, left me with her kidney, and wants to kill me, too; and a child whose caregiver is dead is in my bathtub. Holy shit!*

When she returned to the bathroom, Phoebe tried to wash her hair.

"Let me help you with that," Maddy said. She swirled the shampoo around and rubbed it into the child's scalp. "You have beautiful hair." Using a pitcher, she rinsed out the shampoo and then held up a large bath towel for Phoebe to wrap around herself. "Dry off and put on the nightgown. I made a fire. Come out when you finish, and I'll towel dry your hair." Maddy's emotions were everywhere, and she began feeling a long-forgotten maternal instinct.

Phoebe came out and sat on the floor, and Maddy started brushing and drying her hair. She wanted to ask Phoebe if she had seen the man who killed her grandmother but stopped herself. *I can't imagine what this child has experienced over these last twenty-four hours.*

"That should do it. It's getting late. Come on; I'll show you your room."

After turning back the covers, she watched Phoebe crawl into bed. Maddy pulled the blanket around her and sat close.

"Was this an upsetting day?" she asked. Phoebe lowered her head and nodded. "Were you scared?"

"No, I was sad," she said. That wasn't what Maddy expected.

"What were you sad about?"

"I made Grandma cry." The girl looked at Maddy with curling lips and her eyes watering as she tried to hold back her tears.

"I'd be sad as well. Would you like to talk about it?" Phoebe shook her head. "Well, I'm here to listen if you change your mind. Do you want the nightlight on?" she asked.

"Yes, please."

She flipped the switch on the tiny dresser lamp and turned off the overhead light. "I'll leave the door open, too. Goodnight, Phoebe."

Maddy lay in bed, trying to connect the puzzle pieces that entered her life that day. She always looked for missing parts when confronted with uncertainty. It was how her mind worked and helped her solve the Cupid serial killer case as a detective. She believed the truth hid in the fragments.

Why did Whitfield pick Abigail Hicks to kill? Hannah said he always has a reason. But what is that reason? And why didn't he kill Phoebe? Maybe he didn't realize she lived there. If he finds out, he will undoubtedly think she might expose him and will try killing her, too. Did Phoebe see Whitfield? Jesus, what a mess.

Maddy felt the covers move and a skinny, warm body snuggling up to her back. She said nothing, remained still, and soon heard the child breathing as she drifted asleep.

CHAPTER TWO

The following morning, a breeze from an open window wafted onto Maddy's arm, chilling her as she lay. Afraid of waking Phoebe, she carefully slid out of bed, put on sweat clothes, and pulled a blanket over the child before going to the kitchen. It was no longer night but not quite day, and a grayish-brown haze blocked her view of the mountains. She shuddered at the sight of the pan with the kidney in the refrigerator. She poured water into a pot, scooped in extra coffee to make it strong, and, crossing her arms, leaned back on the counter, waiting for it to percolate. Maddy was thinking of the powerful events of the prior day.

She opened a kitchen window, a lonely bird sang in the distance, and the katydids had stopped chirping; daylight was near. Her mind bounced around as she sat with her coffee at the table. *How much should I tell Adam?* They shared everything, but he was weak from the surgery, and she worried too much stress might hinder his recovery. *And should I tell Hannah Whitfield is taunting me? I won't let them put me under a microscope.* Phoebe preyed upon her mind, too. *I can't keep her here; she'll be in danger. Hannah needs to know.*

Sipping her coffee, she ran through her troubles. She was tired, although the day hadn't started. She left her coffee on the table and drifted off on the sofa. When her eyes opened, Phoebe was standing before her.

"Hi," the girl said, standing in the red dress Maddy had washed for her.

"Oh, hi, sweetie," Maddy said, sitting up, running her fingers through her hair, trying to shake the cobwebs out of her head. The sun shone over the mountain and through the kitchen window. "What time is it?" She glanced at the mantle clock, and it was 9:38.

"Are you hungry?" Phoebe nodded. They walked to the kitchen, and Phoebe stood beside her as she opened the pantry door. "Do you see anything good?" They gazed at several boxes of cereal she'd bought when her grandkids visited a month earlier.

"I like Rice Krispies," Phoebe said.

Maddy reached for the box, brought it to the table, and as Phoebe sat, Maddy grabbed a bowl, spoon, and milk and brought it to her. She reheated the coffee and sat with a cupful, watching her eat.

"What made you come here yesterday?" she asked.

"I got mad at Grandma and ran away." Maddy realized something entirely different had happened than what she'd thought.

"I came to my mother's cross," Phoebe said. "I've been here with Grandma to bring flowers and remembered the way."

"You must have been awful mad to run away," Maddy said.

"I was." Looking at Maddy, she added, "Grandma said I couldn't see Aunt Betsy anymore, and I got mad at her."

Who is Aunt Betsy? Maddy wondered.

"Why didn't she let you see her?" she asked.

"Because they argued. Aunt Betsy thought I should attend school with other kids, but Grandma disagreed. She said she'd never let her see me again. That's why I ran. I tried to find Aunt Betsy's house, but I got lost. I know the way through the woods; my aunt showed me, but the thunder scared me, so I came here."

Maddy listened in amazement as the child rambled. "I said I wanted to go to school and be with other kids. But Grandma got upset. I don't understand why she is being so stubborn."

"What do you plan to do now?" Maddy asked.

"Maybe I'll go back to Grandma's; she's probably worried."

Oh my God, she doesn't know Abigail's dead.

"Why don't you stay here, and we can go together?" Maddy thought it was best to take the girl to her empty house and explain her grandmother's death. The sound of gravel crunching turned both of their heads. A sheriff's cruiser pulled up outside, and Phoebe looked alarmed.

"Stay here; I'll make him go away," Maddy said. She walked out with her arms crossed, and a young guy got out.

"Hi, Ms. Reynolds, I'm Deputy Mott. After what happened to Mrs. Hicks, Sheriff Collins is having us check in with people to be sure they're safe."

"Thank you, Deputy. Everything is fine here."

"Okay, call us if you notice anything unusual." He left, and Maddy returned to the house after he was out of sight.

The Rice Krispies box was on the table. A spoon was in the bowl, and the basement door was open. Phoebe was gone. "Shit!" Maddy went to the door, looked downstairs, and light streamed onto the basement floor. She descended the stairs and looked out at the field. Phoebe was nowhere in sight. Thinking Hannah needed to be informed, Maddy got ready to visit the command center.

Hannah was on the phone when she arrived. She hung up, stood, and crossed her arms as Maddy walked to her.

"What brings you here?" she asked.

"I found your missing body."

"Have a seat," Hannah said.

"The girl is as alive as you and me. She came to the cross behind my home, where they found her mother's body. The storm drove her to my house and into the basement. I coaxed her into staying with me overnight, but a sheriff's cruiser stopped by my place this morning and scared her off. She probably thinks I called the authorities, and I doubt she'll be back."

"Did she give you any information?" Hannah asked.

"She said her name is Phoebe, and she ran away because her grandmother and her Aunt Betsy argued."

"Who's Aunt Betsy?"

"I don't know, but believe it or not, the kid doesn't know her grandmother is dead."

"She'll probably go home to find the place locked up and her grandmother gone," Hannah said.

"The girl may look for a shed or barn to hide in," Maddy said.

Hannah shook her head. "We think Abigail knew her killer. That means Whitfield probably had been to her house at some point. The way Abigail had her granddaughter hidden, I doubt he realized a kid lived there. If he did, he would have killed her too."

"He still might," Maddy said. "If she's in the woods, someone will see her, and the news will spread. Reach her before he does."

"We're working on it," Hannah said. Maddy stood to leave and saw Bates gazing at her. "Is that a handgun you're carrying?" Maddy stopped and lifted the shirt, exposing the Glock.

"It's legal," she said.

"I'm not worried whether it's legal. I'm just wondering why you're carrying."

Maddy hesitated, then flippantly said, "There's a serial killer around town, and I seem to attract them." She smiled and added, "It's just in case."

Maddy went to her Jeep, questioning herself. *Maybe I should have told Hannah that Whitfield is communicating with me. She's not dumb; she knows something's up, and walking into an FBI command center with a weapon was a stupid move.*

Arriving home, she went to her room. She grabbed the ammunition for the Glock. Wrapping it in a towel, she brought it to the back of the house. Dragging a target from the basement, she set it up on a woodpile and counted off seventy-five yards. She loaded, took a deep breath, exhaled, and fired ten times. She walked back to the target.

Holy shit, I can't believe the accuracy I've lost. She returned to try again, reloaded, and aimed. Her hand trembled, and she could not steady herself. "Fuck!"

Frustrated, she sat on the grass, resting her wrists on her knees, thinking of Phoebe. She walked across the field and stepped into the trees. At the wooden cross that marked where they found Luellen Hicks dead years earlier, flowers lay. Water dripped from the freshly cut stems, and Maddy knew her daughter had left them. Her heart ached, and she looked into the woods for Phoebe's red dress.

"Phoebe," she called out. "Are you out there?" No response came. She heard a branch break and shouted again, "Phoebe, are you out there? Come out where I can see you." Two men and a woman walking thirty yards apart from one another approached, and she recognized Hannah's senior agent, Allen Bowers.

"I think we're looking for the same person," he said.

"Yes, her name is Phoebe," Maddy said. "Have you seen any signs of her?"

"We've heard her, but she doesn't want anyone to find her," he said.

Maddy started back, thinking the search party would scare Phoebe and the girl wouldn't return. Crossing the field back to the house, she saw a hawk riding wind currents effortlessly across the sky until it disappeared in the clouds. *I wish I could go with you.*

She brought her handgun and ammunition to the kitchen and poured a glass of orange juice. Wondering how things had gotten so crazy, she grabbed the portable phone and dialed a familiar number at the Oneida County Sheriff's Department.

"Captain Zepatello here." Frank Zepatello had been her boss.

"Zep, have you heard?" she said.

"Yes, the FBI notified us Amos Whitfield is in Berry Lake. Are you alright?"

"No," she said. "He's taunting me."

Zep was a highly respected captain in the Oneida County Sheriff's Office and had led men in battle in Vietnam. He'd selected Maddy to be the first woman detective in the department, and she'd become his protégé.

"Talk to me, Maddy," he said.

"He murdered a local woman, took both of her kidneys and left me one. Sidney Myers thinks he's come to Berry Lake to kill me."

There was silence, and Maddy envisioned Zep getting up and pacing around his office with the phone to his ear, the way he always used to do.

"Are you considering telling the FBI he's communicating with you?" he asked.

"How will they react if I tell them?"

"They'll put surveillance everywhere: your mailbox, your phone, around your house. They'll follow you in your car and be right up your butt."

"I can't handle that," she said. "I've never depended on someone else to keep me safe."

Zep said he understood that part of her. "You've always been like that. Having the FBI protect you is no guarantee you'll be safe; he's outsmarted them before."

"But I'm out of shape, and I haven't touched my weapon in three years," she said.

"Retreat, Maddy, retreat," Zep said. "Become invisible until you're ready for him. The guy's an expert shooter, and you're unprepared to face him. The more he sees you around that town, the more you'll remain top of mind. Stay out of sight until you're ready."

"I've lost my confidence, Zep."

"Get it back," he said. "You can do it. You've done it before. If you take on Whitfield alone, you'll need to whip yourself into shape fast. You have time, but not much. He won't try to take you out immediately. He'll want to impress you by killing more victims first. Use what time you have to prepare." Maddy knew he was right, but it was easier said than done.

"It feels like Cupid all over again," she said. "Why does this keep happening to me?"

"We don't get to choose who we battle, but we can choose how. You're facing a hardened killer. You know how to do it. Remember, there's a killer in you, too, just like me. We keep that part of ourselves hidden because we know it scares people. But that's the part of you that's needed now. Call on the warrior inside and let it guide you; it will save your life."

She sighed, was silent, and finally said, "Thanks, Zep."

"Remember—I'm always here if you need me," he said before they ended the call.

I know what I have to do. Maddy went to her Jeep and started for the village, thinking of Zep's words. She knew the part of herself Zep referred to. *Maybe that part will never be gone.* Pulling over in front of Lester's Hardware Store, she found him in the back.

"Hi, Maddy," he said from behind the counter.

"Hey, Lester, do you still carry ammunition?"

"Sure, what do you need?"

"Nine-millimeter for a Glock."

"I have a few types; hang on." He entered the back room and carried out boxes of three different brands.

"I'll take the Sig Sauer 9mm 115-grain, V-CROWN jacketed hollow points with brass cases."

"Okay, but they're kind of expensive. How many boxes do you want?"

"As many as you have."

"Shit, Maddy, are you looking to go to war?" Lester chuckled.

Maybe I am, she thought.

She drove home, still wondering if she was doing the right thing. *Should I tell Hannah that Whitfield is after me?* Surrendering control of her safety made her stomach tighten. *I'm not ready to do that.*

When she was twelve, her father's death forced her to move from Chicago to Utica to live with her grandmother. She became haunted by the fear his killer might come to kill her, too. Anxiety plagued her. As a young teen, Maddy never went to sleepovers or summer camps. She could not sleep alone; she crawled into her grandma's bed every night.

It wasn't until she learned to shoot that she found the antidote to her troubles. She practiced until she achieved the High Master Shooter ranking at nineteen. She took control of her life, locking away the goblins of her childhood. But the kidney in her mailbox triggered her traumatic past, and the goblins danced in her head the way they did when she was twelve.

When she got home, Maddy prepared to sugarcoat what was happening to Adam. She decided not to put undue stress on his fragile postoperative state by telling him a serial killer was taunting her. She dialed his room, and he answered.

"Hey, it's me," she said.

"Maddy, I was just reading the newspaper about the murder in Berry Lake, but they didn't give the name; who was it?"

"Abigail Hicks," she said.

"Abigail Hicks? Are you kidding? The article said the FBI is involved; what the hell happened?"

"They think Amos Whitfield killed her."

"Whitfield is in Berry Lake? Who told you that?"

"Hannah is leading the investigation," she said. "I saw her at Lena's, and she said Whitfield took Abigail's kidneys."

"Oh, my God. You should get out of town. Visit Jodi in Denver."

"Calm down, Adam, I'm not going anywhere." She heard him sigh and, under his breath, say, "Fuck."

"I can't believe I'm stuck here while you're home alone with Amos Whitfield roaming around Berry Lake," Adam said. "Of course, even if I were there, I couldn't help you. I can barely make it to the bathroom on my own."

"You would make me feel a lot better if you weren't worrying about me and instead focused on the program," Maddy said.

"That's a little hard to do. Think of how you'd feel if you were in my shoes," he said.

"We'll just have to find a way to handle it," she said.

"I know, you're right. Call me every day, okay??"

They said they loved each other. Maddy put her head in her hand when they hung up. *I hate deceiving him.* She remembered Adam's question and realized she might never forgive him if he did the same thing. She redialed his number, and he picked up the phone.

"It's me again. I didn't tell you everything. Whitfield left a kidney in our mailbox." She waited; there was silence, and finally, he spoke.

"He wants to kill you!" he said.

"Yes, I spoke with Sidney Myers, and he thinks that's why he came to Berry Lake."

"Don't tell me; you don't plan to tell the FBI." She didn't speak. "Jesus, Maddy, you're a sitting duck on that mountain alone. What the fuck!"

"Adam, you need to think about what you're saying. I'm not telling the FBI. I just can't put my fate in their hands. I told Zep how I felt, and he suggested I lie low and stay out of sight. Maybe Hannah and her team will get to him, but I'm working on my shooting skills just in case. I'm sorry you feel the way you do. I was hoping you'd understand me better by this point in our relationship," she said.

"I can't believe this," he snapped.

"I think we better hang up before I say things I'll regret later," Maddy said. "Goodbye, Adam."

I'm so pissed at him I could spit, she thought when the conversation ended. She took deep breaths, trying to calm herself, and noticed the message light blinking. She pressed the button, and it was her friend Jodi.

"Hi, it's me. I'm sending you something I bought for you years ago when I was at Cornell," the message said. "It's a cool puzzle I'd forgotten about. My old roommate, Beverly Arnold, has had it all these years. She'll be visiting her parents in Tupper Lake, so she'll drive by your place and said she'd drop it off. I hope you like it. Let's talk soon.

Bye." Maddy was a puzzle enthusiast and had enhanced her detective work by piecing together clues with her puzzle-solving skills.

She pushed herself through the rest of the day with Adam on her mind. By evening, she realized he had said those things because he loved her. *I'll reach out to him tomorrow,* she thought. Maddy didn't believe in letting arguments go unresolved for too long.

CHAPTER THREE

Hannah Bates

Walking around the command center, Hannah wondered how well her team would hold up under what lay ahead. The sun had set, and she went to the coffee table to fill a Styrofoam cup. It was fresh the way she liked and caffeinated, but it didn't matter because she wasn't planning on getting much sleep that night.

Sara, the youngest of her team, called out, "Chief Analyst Benjamin Harris is on the phone for you, Agent Bates." Harris was Hannah's boss.

"Put it through to my desk," she said.

"What's the situation, Hannah?"

"If it's not Whitfield, it's a damn good copycat."

"Have you gotten the forensics report back yet?"

"I'm waiting for Larry to finish with the medical examiner. Here's what we know so far. Witnesses saw the victim leaving the post office alone at about nine-ten. A few kids riding bikes found her body near her car at Blind Bluff at eleven-fifty-six. It's a seven-minute drive, so he had over an hour and a half to kill her, cut her open, and do his thing."

"Do we know where she contacted the killer?" he asked.

"People saw her leave the post office alone. We don't think the perpetrator entered her car, and the only plausible explanation is she met him where the murder took place. She had to know him. Everyone we've interviewed said she was a loner, and no one ever saw her with another person, so it's strange."

"Were there prints or tire tracks?" he asked.

"No fingerprints or DNA," she said. "The road at Blind Bluff has large stones, making it impossible to get a read on tire tracks. We picked up a few where the gravel meets the pavement on the main road, and we have our guys working to identify them, but they are ill-defined. Even if they find something, if Whitfield follows his typical mode of operation, it's a stolen vehicle."

"Let's hope he doesn't go into a killing frenzy," Harris said. "If he does, you'll need more agents. What about the other body?" he asked. Hannah was waiting for that.

"The girl is not dead, Ben. She showed up at Maddy Reynolds' house yesterday during a storm but got scared off this morning. She's out there somewhere in the woods. I'll keep you posted."

When Hannah hung up, Sara walked over with an arm filled with papers.

"This is all the research documentation we had faxed over on Whitfield. Where do you want it?" Hannah nodded to the long table nearby.

"That's where I'll be until morning," she said.

Sara laid the documents on the table, and as Hannah perused the material, Allen Bowers came over and asked if she wanted help.

"No thanks," she said. "I need to get Whitfield figured out. It's easier for me to do it alone. Let's regroup in the morning; there'll be plenty to do."

"Got it," he said.

Hannah pulled up a chair and started sorting through the information. She made piles, murder by murder, organized by the towns where Whitfield had lived. When she finished, she looked around, and the place was quiet, dark, and empty. It was late, and nearly everyone had gone to the cots. She pulled over a stack and started reading when Larry Simmons walked to the table.

"How about a cup of coffee?" Hannah asked.

"No thanks, I'm finding a cot when we're done."

"So, what did you find?" she inquired.

Larry opened a folder, moved a few papers around, and pulled out a document. "According to Tom Hartley, the medical examiner, the perpetrator cut into her abdomen. He had to remove a rib to perform the procedure. He cleanly cut away the ureter and the attached blood vessels from the kidneys before removing them. Under his operating conditions, he did a damn good job. According to Hartley, the incisions are right out of the medical textbooks; the guy has to be a surgeon."

"Did he take any other organs?" she asked.

"Not this time," Larry said.

Hannah sat back in her seat and sipped her coffee.

"I'm trying to figure out why he came to Berry Lake," she said. "Whitfield normally moves into densely populated areas with more opportunities to hide. Maybe he's getting careless or perhaps has another purpose."

"Judging from how he did his post-mortem surgery, the guy appears to be anything but careless," Larry said. "He's meticulously precise."

Hannah folded her arms and said that was what she feared. "You better get some sleep," she said. "I'll see you in the morning."

She returned to examining the information on Whitfield, and reviewed sketches of the man's face. The men in the five drawings appeared as five completely different people. Whitfield was thin sometimes as well as chubby. He had several hair lengths and was occasionally bald. His facial hair varied from clean-shaven to bearded. *The son-of-a-bitch is a master of disguise,* she thought.

She was particularly interested in Whitfield's Michigan killing frenzy. He'd only entered a frenzy twice. The psychiatric explanation was that it starts if he perceives rejection by a woman. In Michigan, the killer had been an auto mechanic. The rapid killing spree began when a female customer complained he'd done shoddy work on her car. They found out later that he had expressed romantic feelings for the woman before her complaint.

It wasn't until a year later that the FBI figured out the incident had triggered the five rapid murders. The woman involved was his last victim, and according to the reports, he tortured her before she died.

Hannah looked around the room, wondering what lay ahead. She was alone and walked outside to get fresh air. She looked over to where the residents of Berry Lake slept in the distance. *They're about to be hit by a hurricane.*

Returning inside, she resumed reading until her eyes grew too heavy. She found an open cot. After finding a comfortable position, she began thinking of Anthony and Charles and peacefully fell asleep.

•   •   •

The following morning, she woke up to voices in the next room. Hannah had slept three hours, and her lower back screamed for mercy as usual when she sat. She showered in the makeshift women's powder room in the girls' gym. Her team was busily working at their positions when she came out. Allen approached her.

"Where do you want me to focus?" he asked. Hannah walked him to her desk and scrolled her list.

"I want you to identify every planned social event over the next six weeks. You should look for county fairs, weddings, reunions, church socials—any gathering. We also need a list of all male residents who arrived in the past four years. Allen scribbled some notes and walked away.

Sara had compiled a listing of police reports and had placed it on Hannah's desk. She shuffled through domestic disputes, stolen cars, bar fights, but one incident caught Hannah's attention. A woman reported that someone had stolen her blueberry pie, which she had left to cool on her back porch.

CHAPTER FOUR

Maddy

A chattering squirrel awakened her, and when she looked up, the clock read 6:40. *That damn thing*, she thought, covering her head with a pillow. Maddy tried falling back asleep but couldn't and forced herself to her feet. She went into the kitchen. Opening the fridge, she saw the kidney in a pan and nearly vomited. *That's going in the basement freezer*, she thought, pushing it to the side.

Grabbing the blueberries and a carton of egg whites, she snacked on the berries, pulled out a frying pan, and lit the burner on the stove. She heated olive oil, tossed in fresh broccoli, added the egg whites and cheddar cheese, and cooked an omelet. *Today, I'll start getting back into shape*, she thought.

It was nearly 8:30 when she stepped into the sunshine. She kneeled, tied her sneakers, and stretched her legs before jogging the hill behind her house. The cool morning air filled her lungs, and her feet dampened as the dew penetrated her sneakers and socks. When she reached the bottom, she stopped and thought it wasn't too difficult, but she was dying halfway back up the hill. Gasping for air, she held her side and had to push to finish the first sprint. Standing with her hands on her hips, sweating, she tried to catch her breath, wondering how she'd let herself get so out of shape.

Only nine more times, she thought. She wanted to run across the field ten times but walked most of it. The sun had reached the top of the mountain and beat on her. When she finished, she sat on the deck, drenched in sweat.

When her body cooled, she grabbed orange juice from the fridge. "Ahh, that's good," she said, drinking from the carton. After showering, Maddy dressed and returned outside for her shooting routine. A refreshing breeze and cloud cover brought relief. Her legs ached, but it was the ache of strengthening muscles, and she didn't mind it.

She was about to begin when a white Saab drove the gravel road to her place and stopped. A tall, pregnant woman in her thirties stepped out.

"Are you Maddy?" the woman asked.

"That's me," Maddy said.

"Special delivery from Jodi Novak," she said, smiling and holding a paper bag.

"You must be Beverly," Maddy said.

"Our mutual friend beckoned me to bring you this unusual puzzle."

The woman's face glowed, and Maddy thought, *She's exactly the person I'd envision Jodi having as a friend.*

"I was about to make lunch. How about joining me?"

"That would be lovely," Beverly said. She started up the deck stairs carrying the bag, obviously straining herself.

"Is that the puzzle?" Maddy asked, reaching for the bag and taking it.

"Oh, thanks," Beverly said as she handed it to her. "Back pain comes with pregnancy, I've learned," she said, laughing.

Maddy led her to the living room and a comfortable chair.

"Would you like a glass of lemonade or ice water?" she asked.

"Ice water will be fine."

Maddy returned with two glasses, set them on the end table, sat, and lifted the bag with the box onto her lap. She pulled out the puzzle and read the title out loud.

"*The Maiden and the Lily*, by, To Ngoc Van," she said, admiring the box cover of a young Vietnamese woman in a long dress, sitting curled over a white lily, gazing.

"That's Jodi," Beverly said.

"She said it makes her think of me, but I think you're right—it's her," Maddy said.

"Well, maybe it represents the part of her she sees in you."

"Spoken like a genuine artist," Maddy said, remembering Jodi telling her of Beverly's artistic gifts.

"Another secret I've learned about being pregnant," Beverly said, "are the frequent trips to the bathroom."

"Down the hall," Maddy said. "I'll start lunch. I hope you like chicken salad sandwiches and tomato soup."

"Perfect," Beverly said. The sandwiches and soup were on the table when she returned to the kitchen. "I love these mountains," Beverly said, looking out the back window. "I've been coming to the Adirondacks as long as I can remember. My parents retired to Tupper Lake, where I'm headed from here.

They sat, and Maddy explained how Jodi turned her on to the region years ago. "Once I saw this flat top mountain, I became obsessed with living on it."

They started eating, and Maddy asked how many months pregnant she was.

"Seven, and won't that make my parents surprised?"

"They don't know?"

"They will tonight," Beverly said, smiling.

"How do you think they'll handle it?"

"I think they'll be happy for me but sad simultaneously." Maddy looked at her as though she didn't understand. "They'll be sad because the baby's father wants nothing to do with it." Beverly lay her soup spoon on a plate, and her eyes watered. She wiped her tears with a napkin and apologized. Maddy put her hand on hers.

"You're a very courageous person having this child alone," she said. "Your parents should be proud of you."

"Thanks," Beverly said.

When they finished with lunch, Maddy walked her to her car. Beverly opened the window to say goodbye, and Maddy noticed a leather necklace with a peace sign hanging from the rear-view mirror.

"I haven't seen one of those in years," she said.

"I'm a hippie at heart," Beverly said.

"I can see that in you."

"Is there a gas station nearby?" Beverly asked. "I meant to gas up in Star Lake but drove right through. I'm getting low."

"There's a Sunoco station about a mile outside Berry Lake," Maddy said. Beverly drove off, as Maddy watched and thought, *What an amazing person.*

•   •   •

Maddy finally called Adam and brought the phone to the deck.

"It's me," she said when he answered.

"I was about to call you," he said. "I hate being mad at each other."

"Me too," she said.

"Let's take the Whitfield thing one step at a time," Adam suggested. "I wish you were with me right now."

Maddy chuckled. "That's not a good idea. There are nosey nurses around."

"I'd use a chair to block the door," he said.

"Yeah, but they would hear us," she said.

"True, but who cares?"

"I love you, Adam Forsyth," she said.

"I love you too, Maddy Reynolds."

They sighed and said goodbye.

•   •   •

Maddy had gone to bed early, but the phone rang at 12:05 AM, waking her. She thought it was the hospital and ran to answer.

"Ms. Reynolds?" a man said, sounding alarmed.

"Yes, this is Maddy Reynolds," she said.

"This is Peter Arnold, Beverly Arnold's father. I'm sorry for calling so late, but my wife and I are beside ourselves worrying about our daughter. She mentioned she was stopping by your house on her way here. Did she?"

"Yes, she did."

"What time did she leave?" he asked.

"She left here about three-fifteen this afternoon. Hasn't she arrived?"

"No, she hasn't," he said. Maddy asked if he'd called the police, and he said he hadn't.

"We thought maybe she stopped somewhere else along the way. We've called her cell phone, but she hasn't picked up."

"I think you need to call the sheriff, Mr. Arnold."

"Okay, I'll call when I hang up with you," he said.

Maddy walked to the living room with folded arms. She glimpsed the Maiden and the Lily puzzle on the dining room table. *Where could she be?* She looked into the darkness from the kitchen window. *She's out there somewhere; maybe she ran out of gas.*

Running her fingers through her hair, it hit her—*Whitfield!* She paced around her place, thinking of the serial killer, and nearly wept at the thought that Beverly might be in his grip. Finally, she sat on the sofa, put her weapon on the coffee table, and drifted off, listening to the night sounds outside an open window. She jumped up when the phone rang again, and she answered.

"Maddy, this is Hannah Bates. I realize it's the middle of the night, but I'd like to come to your home. It's about Beverly Arnold."

"I'll put on coffee," Maddy said.

She headed to the kitchen and started brewing coffee. She gazed outside at a crescent moon reflecting on the lake. *Usually, I'd think it was beautiful,* she thought, *but now it feels ominous.* Hannah's call hinted that the FBI suspected Whitfield's involvement in Beverly's disappearance.

Before the pot percolated, headlights lit the trees behind her house, and a car pulled up. Maddy greeted Bates and Bowers at the back door.

"Sorry to have to do this, Maddy," Hannah said as she stepped inside with Allen Bowers behind her. "We got a call from Beverly Arnold's father, who said you were the last person to speak with her."

"That's okay," Maddy said. "Have a seat in the living room."

Hannah and Allen went inside and sat, and Maddy brought a tray with the coffee.

"Beverly came here about one o'clock this afternoon," Maddy said as she sat down. "She's friends with my friend Jodi, and she brought me a gift from her on the way to visit her parents."

"How long did she stay?" Hannah asked.

"She left about three-fifteen."

"Did she mention making any stops before getting to Tupper Lake?" Allen asked.

"She said she needed gas soon. I told her about the Sunoco outside of town."

"That gas station is closed for repairs," Allen said. "We had to send our vehicles to Star Lake to fill up today."

"Oh, my God. She must have run out," Maddy said. She put her head in her hands, thinking of the lovely Beverly. "What are the chances Whitfield came upon her?"

"He normally knows his victims and grooms them for weeks before he kills them," Hannah said. "The only time he's gone cruising for his prey is when he's in a killing frenzy."

"What are your next steps?" Maddy asked.

"It will be dawn soon. We'll use helicopters to search along the roadsides. Let's hope for the best. Maybe she'll turn up okay."

When they drove off, it was still dark, and Maddy couldn't get Beverly's baby bump out of her mind. *If it's Whitfield, he'll take the fetus.* The thought gnawed at her. *I know this feeling. It's the same as I've had with the other crazy bastards who prey on people weaker than themselves.* "Fuck," she screamed at the mountains with her fists clenched as she walked back to the house.

With each step, she was moving into another part of herself, the part Zep referred to. Any doubts about telling Hannah that Whitfield was communicating with her were gone. *He's come here for me, and I'm not fucking running.*

Maddy shut and locked the sliding glass door and brought her weapon to the coffee table again. *I need rest!*

•   •   •

Her eyes opened when the house shook from a helicopter's rapid thuds rattling the dishes. She sat. *They're looking for Beverly.* The phone rang, and it was a Denver number. *It's Jodi.* She grabbed the receiver and said hello.

"Maddy, what happened?" Jodi shouted. "I just got a call from Beverly's sister, and she said Beverly is missing."

"It's true. She never made it to her parents after she left my house. The FBI is looking for her."

"Why the FBI?" Jodi asked. "Is that killer involved?"

"It's possible," Maddy said.

"Oh my God, her family doesn't know that. I feel so terrible."

"It's not your fault, Jodi." Jodi fearfully sighed and said how unreal the situation seemed.

"I know," Maddy said. "It's hard to believe."

They said they'd stay in touch before ending the call. Feeling overwhelmed, Maddy headed to Lena's hoping the familiar place might be comforting. Julie Barnes, Marjorie Best, and Reverend Dietrich sat at a booth when she entered the diner. "Hey, Maddy," Julie called out.

"Hi, guys," Maddy said.

"Did you hear there's another victim?" Julie said.

"I heard someone is missing, but not a victim."

"Yes, Maddy, you're right," Reverend Dietrich said. "Let's not jump to conclusions, least we lose our faith all together."

Ernie Bajorek walked by as he was leaving the diner and hesitated when he saw Marjorie.

"Hello, Marjorie," he said, smiling, looking directly at her. He suddenly noticed the others, blushed, and said, "Hi, everyone," before walking away.

Julie teasingly asked Marjorie what that was all about.

"Knock it off," Marjorie said.

"Let's not forget ourselves, ladies," the Reverend said admonishingly.

"Sorry, Reverend," Julie said with a smile.

"Do you know the missing woman, Maddy?" Dietrich asked.

"She's a friend of a friend."

"Is it true Abigail Hicks had a young girl living with her, and the kid went to your house?" Julie asked. *News spreads fast in this town.*

"Yes, it's true," Maddy said.

"Where is she now?" asked the reverend.

"Scared off, and I suspect she's hiding in the woods."

"The poor thing," Dietrich said.

Maddy politely walked away to sit at the counter. Screeching tires, revved engines, and a half-dozen law enforcement vehicles speeding in the same direction outdoors caused her to walk to the window.

They found Beverly! She hurried to her Jeep and followed.

Two miles beyond the Sunoco station, a cavalry of law enforcement huddled on the side of the road, gazing down a hill.

Maddy pulled over fifty yards away, got out, and watched. She saw Hannah Bates pointing and directing the others. More official vehicles arrived, and Tom Hartley, the medical examiner, got out of a black, windowless van. The white-haired man slipped on a blue protective gown over his street clothes and masked his face. Two FBI agents helped Hartley down the hill as Hannah followed, and they disappeared out of sight.

Time passed, and finally, the two agents helped Hartley onto the road with Bates behind them. The medical examiner removed his protective gear, and the man's face was as white as his hair. *He must have seen something horrific,* Maddy thought. Hannah's eyes looked straight ahead. She wasn't paying attention to her surroundings as she stepped onto the road; her mind seemed far off. *I can't imagine what she's thinking right now.*

The winch motor on a tow truck started running; it strained, and the weeds moved as men guided a white Saab onto the road. *Beverly must have run out of gas,* Maddy thought with tears in her eyes. Men carried a body bag up the hill. *I can't believe this is happening,* she thought, turning and entering her Jeep.

Clouds hid the sun, the mountains were dull and gray, and a heavy numbness filled her chest as she drove home. *The man coming here to kill me killed Beverly and her baby. Who is this monster I must face?*

She arrived at her house and went inside, not wanting to talk with anybody; she only wanted to be left alone. On her way to her bedroom, she glimpsed the *Maiden and the Lily* puzzle. *I thought I could relax and put that together this summer,* she cynically said to herself.

She spent the day in her room, lying on the bed. Hours passed, and the light dimmed outside her window. She sat up and went to the kitchen pantry, pulled out a bottle of Cabernet, uncorked it, and brought it to the deck with a goblet. It was late afternoon; the clouds had covered the sun, and a cool breeze from across the lake chilled her. She sipped the wine, and the scent of wood burning somewhere in the distance reminded her of the night The Glades burned.

Why is my life this way? As hard as she'd tried to find peace, death and sorrow followed wherever she went. *A killer came for me and took Abigail and Beverly's lives.*

The darkness came, and a loon's wailing made her sad, reminding her of loved ones lost to violence. Her insides ached as pain seeped into her body.

With the wine bottle empty, Maddy lay limp in the darkness, and her mind flashed to the beginning of her woes—the night Cupid killed her father. "Oh, Dad, why was it this way for us?" she said aloud with her arms wrapped around her stomach, her anguish too great. She leaned to her side, curled into a ball, and wept herself to sleep on the deck sofa.

A sound in the woods awakened her, and she sat. It was dark, and she couldn't see. She listened, but the sound didn't repeat. Feeling around with her hand beneath her, she tried to locate the weapon and instead picked up a throw blanket.

What the heck? She assumed she was too drunk to remember going inside for it. Maddy found the weapon, walked inside, and locked the door. She noticed something on the kitchen table, switched on the light, and saw an empty carton of ice cream and a spoon on the table.

My God, Phoebe was here.

CHAPTER FIVE

Hannah

At the Beverly Arnold murder scene, Hannah observed as the crime team led by Eric Tremble gathered evidence. She told Tremble she wanted to see the body.

"We're bringing the medical examiner down now," he said. "You can come along." Hannah and Allen followed two of Tremble's men as they held the elderly medical examiner's arms. Each time Hartley stumbled, the men steadied him.

As Hannah prepared for the gruesome scene, the sun beat on her face, sweat beaded on her forehead, and flies buzzed around her head. When she reached the Saab, her stomach tightened at the sight of congealed blood splattered on the driver's door panel.

"Where's the body?" Hartley asked. Tremble pointed to tall grass a dozen feet away. Helping the old medical examiner through the thicket, two agents walked ahead of Hannah and Allen. When they reached the body, Hannah froze.

A thirty-ish-year-old, brown-haired woman lay on her back, her abdominal and thoracic cavities open wide. Flies feasted on her insides, and blood that had oozed from a hole in her throat caked around her neck. Her eyes bugged out in horror, and an umbilical cord lay flopped on her blood-soaked shirt.

"Over there are the liver and heart," Tremble said. He pointed to two brown organs in the dirt six feet away, where flies feasted.

"Where's the fetus?" Hannah asked. Tremble said it was gone. "Oh my God, it must have been alive when he took it," she said. She heard retching and saw Allen turn away to vomit. Hannah's stomach constricted, and her throat tightened as she covered her mouth.

"Allow the medical examiner to do his job," Tremble said. He directed Allen and Hannah to move to the side. Hannah watched the older man kneeling, easing the woman's insides from side to side. Beverly's expression at the moment of death haunted her.

When Hartley finished and was preparing to leave the body, Hannah's stomach was on the verge of giving up the bagel she had eaten for breakfast. She followed the men carrying the body. Cars had pulled over, people stood watching in the distance, and Maddy Reynolds was among them, leaning back against her Jeep with her arms folded. Hannah thought her look was rage.

"Here they come," Allen said, pointing to four men carrying a black body bag up the hill. When they reached the top, they laid the body on a gurney, strapped it, and slid it into the back of the medical examiner's van. Hannah saw Reynolds driving away. With the body removed from the scene, Tremble walked to where Hannah and Allen stood to give his preliminary findings.

"The Saab pulled over," Tremble said. "There's a second set of tire tracks in front of it."

"Wait," Hannah said. "Didn't she run out of gas?"

"No, she had over a gallon in her tank. The killer must have followed her to this location and somehow waved her over. Size thirteen work boot footprints reveal that a man got out of his car and walked back to the victim's driver's side. It looks like he killed her as she rolled down the window, blood splattered on the handle. He did it quickly; he knew what he was doing."

Tremble wiped the sweat from his forehead with a handkerchief. "The killer pushed the car to the hill. Gravity did the rest. Once he pulled his car into the high weeds, out of sight from the road, he worked unimpeded until he finished. After dragging the body out of the vehicle, he lay it in the weeds, removed her liver and heart, and left them near her."

"The girl was about twenty-three weeks pregnant, and you're right. The fetus was alive when he took it. It took place within an hour," Tremble said.

"How about prints?" Hannah asked.

"None! We've taken samples to test for hair follicles and DNA. He left tire tracks and footprints—plenty of footprints. It's almost like he wanted us to find them. The girl didn't see it coming," he said. He turned and walked away, wiping his head with his handkerchief.

Hannah, Allen, Sara, and another agent spoke no words as they drove back to the command center together. It was early evening, and the sun peaked through the trees. Everyone was in private thoughts, and gloom hung in the car as Allen drove through the village. People were outside strolling, seemingly without care and unaware of the second murder in their town. Hannah imagined the place after the news spread.

Walking into the elementary school, the smell of fish waiting in the cafeteria hit them. They looked at one another.

"I'm going to be sick," Sara said as she ran to the lady's room. Hannah turned around and went outside to breathe the fresh air. Standing alone, trying to control her emotions, she waited, then finally called home.

"Hello, Anthony," she said. He said hello, but she froze and went silent. Finally, her voice cracked when she said she missed him.

"Oh, Hannah, what have you seen?" he said. She wept, wishing she could transport herself into his arms.

"You wouldn't believe me if I told you," she said.

"You can tell me."

"I'd rather not," she said. "It was the saddest, most gruesome scene I could ever imagine. I have to hold myself together for my team. They're all young, and they are reeling. Just tell me a story; tell me something about our son."

"Well, let's see. Charles came home all excited today. He started his lifeguard job at the park pool for the summer and left to see *Independence Day* with his friends. It's been a very wonderful day for him."

"I'll try to hold on to that thought," she said. "I needed to hear that." She glanced over and saw Allen sitting alone at a picnic table. "I have to go."

She walked to where Allen sat. He was holding his stomach and looking at the ground.

"Hey," she said, sitting next to him. "How are you holding up?" He shook his head.

"The sight of that girl is stuck in my head. My wife is pregnant, too. To see her lying there like that—" he started choking up and stopped. Hannah couldn't get the image of Beverly Arnold out of her head, either.

Birds sang, and a slight breeze blew in off the lake.

"It's hard to believe a place so lovely can have such horrific happenings taking place," Hannah said. She looked at his distress, searching for the right words.

"We sign up for field work to pursue our ideals. We hope to create a better world. But we can become cynical once we see the evil humans can do. If it happens, we become part of the problem."

Allen had his arms crossed as though he were holding in his pain. He looked away from Hannah toward the lake. "I've been questioning whether I'm cut out for this work," he said. "I'm not strong like you. I'm not sure how I'll do when my time comes."

"Making a difference doesn't require being a mountain, Allen. We're not meant to be mountains. We all need each other. I couldn't do what I do without agents like you. And when it's your time to face an enemy, you'll be ready. You need to trust that."

"But Hannah, I'm afraid. I look at what this guy is capable of, and I'm scared."

"If you stop being scared, it's time to quit," she said. "I'm scared too. Do you not think that Maddy Reynolds gets scared? We can channel fear into action. I have great confidence in you, Allen."

"Thanks," he said. He waited momentarily and added, "I can feel the tension building in this town. It's like a violin string about to pop. It's surprising how many bad things happened in this small place."

"I know," she said. "I've been wondering about that, too."

They stood and started walking into the building. "I've got to call home," he said.

That night, Hannah was up late again, alone, thinking. *Most of Whitfield's killings have been with victims he'd groomed over time and had gained their trust. But Beverly Arnold appears to be random, a murder of opportunity unless he had another reason we don't know.*

She lay her pen on the desk, pushed back in her chair, and before going to her cot, she thought, *Is it possible Arnold's murder wasn't random?*

CHAPTER SIX

Maddy

Maddy woke up with a hangover, sat up in bed, and thought, *I've got to cut that shit out, or I'll make it real easy for Whitfield to kill me.* She dragged herself to the kitchen to make coffee and saw the empty ice cream container. *I forgot she was here last night. Phoebe must be coming around. I'll start leaving her food and water.*

When her brain started functioning, she threw on shorts and a tee shirt and started her workout routine. It had become a morning ritual, and she knew it might save her life.

"One more time up this damn hill," Maddy huffed, pushing to finish the tenth and final sprint. Her heart pounded, and her legs felt rubbery when she finished. She collapsed and lay on the grass, facing the sun with her head splitting. Sitting up, she looked around and reached for a jug of ice water. What she couldn't drink, she poured over her head.

A brown Dodge pulled up in front, and Hannah Bates got out alone.

"Getting in shape?" Hannah said as she walked to her.

"Have a seat," Maddy said. She got up and walked to the deck.

"Nice day," Hannah said.

"Yeah, great." Maddy knew Hannah wanted to fish for information.

"I saw you at the murder scene yesterday."

"Yup, I was there."

"You know how sometimes things don't jive in an investigation, leaving your mind wandering, looking for answers?" Hannah said. Maddy laughed.

"Is your mind wandering, Hannah?"

"Yes, it is."

"Why don't you tell me your concerns, and maybe I can help."

"Remember how you said Beverly probably ran out of gas? Well, she didn't. She had enough for another 20 miles."

"What's your point?"

"We think Whitfield followed her before pulling her over to the side of the road with his vehicle. Maybe he was near your place when Beverly left."

"What are you getting at?"

"Nothing particular. It's just that I noticed you carrying your weapon the other day. I see you whipping yourself into shape today, and there's a possibility Whitfield followed Beverly Arnold from your place when she left here."

"What does that all add up to?" Maddy asked.

"Maybe it means Whitfield has been coming around your place."

"Now, why would he do that?"

"I'm not sure. Maybe he's showing off."

"Maybe."

Hannah gave her a suspicious smirk before she said, "Did you, by chance, get a glimpse inside Beverly's car?"

"I did," Maddy said.

"We'd like you to stop by the command center. There are items from inside her vehicle we want you to see."

"Has Whitfield started taking trophies other than body parts?" Maddy asked.

"We're not sure. He's deviating from his typical patterns in several ways."

"I'll come by this afternoon," Maddy said.

Hannah started for her car but stopped and looked at Maddy. "I see your target out back. Are you brushing up on your shooting skills, too?" She smiled and walked away.

•   •   •

It was after two in the afternoon when Maddy started for the command center. The first person she saw when she stepped inside was Allen Bowers.

"Hannah will be glad to see you," he said. "Have a seat. She'll be right back." Maddy noticed a document on Hannah's desk entitled *Men new to Berry Lake within the last four years, not yet cleared*. Among the names were Stanley Hartman and Ernie Bajorek.

"Oh, hi, Maddy," Hannah said when she came to her desk. She walked around, sat at her desk, and covered the list of names with a stack of documents. "Thanks for coming by. I have the photos I'd like you to look at." She reached for a large envelope, pulled out glossy-colored pictures, and handed a few to Maddy.

The first photo showed Beverly lying on her back with her eyes wide, frozen in fear, and her chest and abdomen spread wide. "So, he took her fetus," Maddy said, feeling her insides boiling with rage.

The next photo Hannah handed her was of the woman's hands.

"Do you notice any rings or bracelets missing?"

"No," Maddy said.

The third set was of Beverly's clothing — a torn, blood-soaked Cornell tee shirt, blue jeans, a bra, and underwear that hung from a bush. Maddy said she noticed nothing missing. Hannah handed her a fourth stack.

"These are from inside the car."

She saw blood on the driver's door panel, the inside windshield, and the seat. Maddy clenched her fists. "That motherfucker!"

"Do you see anything missing?" Hannah asked.

"Yes, there was a leather necklace with the peace sign hanging from the rear-view mirror."

Hannah crossed her arms. "So, he's changed his behavior. I wonder what it means," she said. Maddy didn't offer a theory, but she suspected it had something to do with her.

"Thanks, I appreciate you doing this," Hannah said.

Maddy got up to leave but stopped. "Has there been any sign of Phoebe?"

"Yes and no," Hannah said. "No one has seen her, but we know she's around. Residents have reported missing food items from porches and root cellars." Shaking her head, Maddy wondered how long before Whitfield found the girl and killed her.

•   •   •

Driving home with a chokehold on the steering wheel, Maddy was thinking of the photos. *Whitfield followed Beverly from my place. He must be hovering near my house,* she thought. She pulled onto the road to her home, resting her hand on the weapon, and carried it to the house when she got out. She noticed something hanging from the back door handle when she stepped onto the deck. It was Beverly's necklace. Adrenaline kicked in, and she snapped around, wielding the Glock.

Concerned that Whitfield found a way inside, she stepped through her place, room by room. She saw the puzzle, and a pang of pain struck her. When she finished, the phone rang.

"Nice house," a muffled voice said before a click and a dial tone.

Suddenly, Maddy was twelve again when haunting shadows appeared in her room, and she'd run to her grandma's bed. She called them shadow monsters. But now they were real. They were shadows of a man seeking to kill her and add another notch to his belt.

Her heart raced. *Whitfield wants me to know he can kill me at will. Calm down, Maddy. You're not twelve; you've been here. He's trying to intimidate you.*

Wrestling with her demons, she tried shoving them back into the box where she kept her childhood fears. *He's not magical; he's human, and you can kill him,* she told herself. *Remember, there's a killer in you, too.*

CHAPTER SEVEN

Marjorie Best

Marjorie stopped by her husband's hardware store before visiting her friend Julie Barnes. The door chimes sounded as she entered. Lester was working on a bent window screen in the back.

"We're taking up a collection for Abigail to have a proper burial," she said. "I think the business should be generous."

"How much?" he asked.

"Fifty." He scowled but said nothing more. "Good, I'm putting you down for fifty dollars." She noted her book and said she was heading to *Things Forgotten* to see Julie next. "I'll see you this evening; we're having chicken and biscuits for dinner. Love you."

She walked two doors to her friend's antique shop. "Morning, Julie, how are you?" The woman was dusting the antiques near the front of the store.

"Not well," Julie said. She stood with the feathered duster in her hand, crossed her arms, and shook her head. "Since they confirmed the missing girl from Tupper Lake was murdered, I can hardly sleep."

"I know," Marjorie said. "Lester left his shotgun in the bedroom last night. It feels just like the summer The Glades burned; very creepy."

"Poor Abigail," Julie said. "She'd grown so isolated since Luellen died. I kept telling myself I'd visit her but never did. Does she have any family at all?"

"No, and that's the reason for my visit. We're fundraising for her burial and headstone. She had few resources. She lived on Social Security. I was hoping I could count on you for twenty-five dollars."

"Yes, I can do twenty-five. How else can I help?

"A few of us are meeting at seven o'clock at Reverend Dietrich's house tonight. Why don't you join us?" Julie said she'd be there.

"I'll pass by your house on my way, so why don't we walk together?"

"Sounds good," Julie said.

"Can you think of anyone else interested in helping?" Marjorie asked.

"Why don't you try Stanley Hartman? He opened the tailor shop across from Lena's. I think he's a widow. He's quiet, but maybe he's looking to make new friends."

"I'll stop by his shop," she said. "How about Maynard Krantz? Do you think he might contribute?"

"Marjorie, that guy hasn't changed since high school. He's a grump. Try him, but when he's not fixing a chimney during the day, he's at Blake's Bar getting pie-eyed. Since his wife left him, I've heard he's gotten worse."

Marjorie had a soft spot for Maynard since high school but didn't mention it. "I might try him," she said. Before saying goodbye, she said she'd see her at 6:45 that evening.

Marjorie walked the street to Lena's and sat in an empty booth, and Rose came over to take her order.

"How are you doing?" Rose asked as she placed a glass of water in front of her.

"I feel so devastated by what happened to poor Abigail," Marjorie said. "She's all I think about. First, her daughter gets murdered, and now her. Some people experience so many awful things." She sighed and ordered a BLT and a Coke.

As she waited for her food, Stanley Hartman, the tailor, was leaving, and she got up to introduce herself. "Hi, Mr. Hartman. I'm Marjorie Best; my husband owns the hardware store." She stuck out her hand; he smiled and took it. He stared at her while she waited for him to let it go, and finally, she pulled her hand away.

"You must have heard about what happened to Abigail Hicks," she said. Hartman's mind seemed elsewhere. "She died, and we are asking for donations for her burial. Would you like to contribute?"

He kept his eyes glued on her as though he were looking through her clothes, and Marjorie felt uncomfortable. He reached into his pocket, pulled out bills, peeled off a dollar, and handed it to her. As he walked out, Marjorie snapped, "Aren't you the generous one?" He turned and glared at her. Rose was walking by with an arm full of dirty dishes and stopped.

Hartman walked out, and Rose leaned over and said to Marjorie, "He's as tight as a soda pop top. He never leaves me a tip."

"I can't believe how strange that man is," Marjorie said.

She finished at Lena's, walked Main Street, and saw Maynard Krantz's truck parked in front of the garage where he housed his chimney sweep business. She gazed inside, saw him cleaning equipment, walked in, and he froze.

"Hi, Marj," he said.

"Hello, Maynard." They awkwardly looked at each other.

"Have you heard what happened to Abigail Hicks?" she asked.

"Yes, I heard. It's too bad. She was a good person who endured a lot of heartache. At least now it's over," he said. Marjorie didn't respond, knowing his comment hinted at his misery.

"Some of us are trying to raise money to buy her a gravestone," she said. "Would you like to contribute?"

He walked to the cash register on the workbench, pulled out three ten-dollar bills, and handed them to her.

"That's all I can do." She thanked him and turned to leave.

"Please don't go, Marj." She stopped, and he walked to her. "Can we talk?"

"We've been through this, Maynard. I married Lester; he's my husband. Our time has passed." He put his hand on her arm, and she looked at him.

"Hearing you say 'I do' to Lester in that church ended my life. I never loved Nancy and made her life miserable until she left me. If I were stronger, I would have left her earlier." Marjorie lowered her head.

"I'm sorry, but I can't change that." Seeing his tears, she walked away.

"Marj!" he shouted. She stopped but didn't turn. "Okay, I'll pretend for you, but I can't lie to myself." Walking out with her eyes watering, she knew he meant they still loved each other.

Marjorie removed her shoes and lay on the sofa when she arrived home. Emotionally drained, her mind was everywhere: Abigail, Stanley Hartman, but mainly Maynard. She always loved him but never told a soul. He was her only lover besides her husband. Afraid of a life of financial struggles, she ended it when they were young. Lester had inherited his father's store and had a mind for business with no vices. He wasn't romantic, but she knew if she married him, she'd have security. Yet, at moments such as that, her insides wept.

She fell asleep, and when she awoke, she made dinner. Lester came home, and they ate without saying a word. He grabbed a beer when he finished eating and went to the couch to watch television while Marjorie cleaned up in the kitchen.

"I'm going upstairs to get ready for a meeting at Reverend Dietrich's," she said. Lester glanced at her. It was 6:30. Lester hadn't moved when she returned to the living room.

"I should be home by about nine-thirty," she said. When she walked outside, the sky was pink, but the mountains hid the sun, and long shadows stretched over the town. When she arrived at Julie's, she was waiting.

"Herb, Marjorie's here; I'm leaving." The two women started walking toward the town center, where Reverend Dietrich lived behind the chapel.

"Well, after I left you, I ran into Stanley Hartman at Lena's," Marjorie said. "What a cheapskate. He begrudgingly gave me a dollar for the fund."

"Did you ask anyone else?" Julie asked.

"I stopped by Maynard's garage, and he gave me thirty dollars."

Julie said nothing. When they reached the reverend's, Marjorie knocked, and he came to the door.

"Come in, ladies. Ernie, can you find chairs for Marjorie and Julie? This town has more warm-hearted people than any other I've lived in."

"Oh, crap, it's Ernie Bajorek," Marjorie whispered.

"I told you he likes you," Julie said. The guy unfolded two chairs and waited as Julie and Marjorie walked over and sat. He looked at Marjorie, smiled, and walked away.

"They say he's wealthy—a retired Wall Street executive," Julie chuckled.

"Thanks a lot," Marjorie said.

"It's not my fault you attract all the men," Julie said. "It's always been that way."

"Settle in now, everyone," Dietrich said as he stood before eighteen townspeople. "We all know why we are here. Let us begin with a brief prayer." He closed his eyes and lowered his head.

"Lord, we have come to you about our deceased sister, Abigail Hicks. She was kind and unassuming, and although she had fallen away from the church in recent years, we know you will welcome her home through your loving kindness. Please bless our efforts to raise money for a place to mark her time on earth. Thank you. Amen."

Dietrich explained that the fundraising goal was twelve hundred dollars. He went around the room asking for the amounts of each person's pledges; the total was six hundred and fifty-seven dollars.

"Wonderful," he said. "We're already more than halfway, and we just started."

They discussed ideas of whom to approach, the gravestone, and the ceremony. They finished, and the reverend told everyone he was proud of his congregation. "I can't wait to write Mrs. Dietrich and tell her what she has to look forward to when she meets you all." His wife was doing missionary work in Africa.

"Rose Gilly made cookies, so please stay and enjoy," Dietrich said.

"Rose makes the most delicious baked goods," Julie said. In the kitchen, they each filled a plate with various types. As they started for the living room to mingle, Reverend Dietrick stopped them.

"Ladies, I want to remind you we've started a prayer group on Wednesday evenings at seven. We are meeting here, and I'm hoping to increase our numbers. Please consider attending."

When the Reverend left them to tell the others of the prayer group, Ernie Bajorek stopped Marjorie. Julie went to the next room.

"Hello, Marjorie," he said. The man was tall and lean, with short hair and wire-rimmed glasses. He fit the image of a Wall Street executive. "These cookies are outrageous, aren't they?" he said as he took a bite. "Is it true your husband owns the hardware store?" he asked.

"Yes, it's been in his family for years."

"That's what I like about a small town—its history. My hometown is constantly changing," he said.

"What made you move here?" she asked.

"My wife hated New York City and wanted to move as far away as possible. So, here we are."

"Is that what *you* wanted?"

Oh shit, I wish I didn't ask him that. He appeared ready to share his deep feelings; she saw it in his eyes.

"To be honest—" he said, but Marjorie cut him off as Julie walked by, and she grabbed her arm. "We should go, don't you think?" Marjorie said.

"Oh, yes, you're right. It's getting late," Julie said.

"It was nice talking to you," Marjorie said to Ernie as she turned to walk away with Julie.

"Hang on," Ernie said. "Would you like to have coffee sometime?" Marjorie looked at him directly.

"Ernie, you're very nice, but we're both married. I'm not comfortable with that. I'm sorry."

"Well, you ladies have quite a long way to walk home, especially you, Marjorie. Why not let me escort you?"

"We'll be fine," Marjorie said. "Thank you anyway." She headed for the door. "The guy doesn't enjoy taking no for an answer," she told Julie as they stepped into the night air. Their exit was a cue for others to leave. The place emptied. It was a warm evening but very dark; a slight breeze blew through the trees.

"Do you think you might attend that prayer group?" Julie asked.

"I don't think so." Julie said she might go.

"Oh dear. Let's cross the street. I think that's Maynard standing in front of Blake's Bar," Marjorie said. They crossed over, and as they passed, loud country music blared as a few men stood outside holding beer bottles. Marjorie kept her head straight.

"That was Maynard," Julie said.

"I know. He's probably drunk." Marjorie said nothing more. They reached Julie's house, and Julie asked if she wanted Herb to walk her home.

"It's only another couple hundred yards; I'll be fine. Good night, Julie."

Marjorie walked into the blackness, and the wind picked up when she was halfway to her house. The only sound was the rustling of leaves, and she regretted not having Julie's husband with her. Her eyes blurred as dust blew into her face. She stopped to rub them, when the full force of a man's body knocked her off her feet and shoved her into the weeds. She tried to scream, but a hand over her mouth stopped her. His other hand reached for the top of her shirt, pulling and ripping it. She felt the man's gloves scraping her neck and chest as he pulled at her blouse.

Squirming to free herself, she resisted, but he used more force, and she realized there was no chance. Moving her body, trying to get her into a particular position, she felt him reach for something in his back pant pocket. *I'm going to die.*

Another body slammed into her attacker, and she heard grunting and fighting. She got free, struggled to her feet, and ran to her house, screaming.

"Someone attacked me," she said when she ran into the house. "I think he wanted to kill me." Lester jumped off the sofa with a horrified look. "Call the sheriff," she screamed. She headed to the kitchen, he to the phone. Looking at herself in the mirror, she splashed water on scratch marks on her neck and chest. Her husband came over, helped her to the living room sofa, and held her.

"What happened?" he asked.

"I…I…I…," she couldn't speak; she just cried.

Cars pulled up in front, Sheriff Collins stepped inside, and behind him, two men in suits and a tall woman in a pantsuit stood.

"These are FBI agents," Collins said. "They've set up a command center in the elementary school, and this is Agent in Charge Hannah Bates." Bates sat next to Marjorie and held her hand.

"Please try to explain what happened, Mrs. Best." Marjorie regained control and wiped her face with a tissue.

"I was returning from a meeting at Reverend Dietrich's, and a man attacked me about seventy-five yards from my house." The other FBI agents bolted from the room, and the sheriff followed.

"Did he try to rape you?" Bates asked.

"I don't think so. I think he wanted to kill me. He kept moving me around like he wanted to do something, but someone jumped on him, and I got free and ran home."

"Who was at the meeting?" Hannah asked. She started taking their names when the sheriff burst into the room, out of breath, and shouted, "It's Maynard Krantz!"

"Krantz did this?" Lester yelled.

"Maynard would never hurt me," Marjorie screamed back at him.

"Maynard is dead," the sheriff said. "Someone cut his throat."

"I think that man saved your life," Hannah said.

A pang of pain struck Marjorie's heart. The man she'd secretly loved since high school had just given up his life for hers.

CHAPTER EIGHT

Marjorie

Marjorie lay in bed the next day, holding a crinkled handkerchief to her face. Her heart was hurting worse than her body. Lester had closed the hardware store and was doing his best to pamper her. She felt guilty because he believed her distress was from the incident, but her thoughts were on Maynard.

He must have followed me from Blake's, wanting to talk. Maynard had approached her several times over the years. He claimed he wanted to talk, but she knew he desired more. Once, she had indulged him in conversation; he kissed her, and she knew she couldn't let it happen again.

Marjorie was an attractive woman who tried to hide her sexuality. She always kept her hair tied up and wore loose-fitting blouses to hide her large breasts. She married an older man who wasn't romantic and convinced herself that the lack of a sex life wasn't a concern. Yet, whenever she'd been around Maynard, she felt disquieted and knew something she needed was missing.

Not wanting to stay in bed all day, she got up. She showered, dressed, and went downstairs. Lester was at the table, writing and talking on the phone. She went to the fridge, poured a glass of orange juice, and sat across from him.

"That was Hannah Bates," he said when he hung up. "She wants to interview you again."

"Did she say when that would be?"

"She said she'd be here around noon," Lester said. "You've gotten phone calls from Julie Barnes and Reverend Dietrich asking how you're doing. I told them you'd call them back later. Are you in pain?"

"My back and neck are sore; otherwise, I'm alright." She sensed Lester struggling to find comforting words and touched his hand as if to say, 'It's okay.'

"I'll be fine if you want to head into the store," she said. "It's probably not a good idea for people to see it closed."

"Are you sure you'll be alright?" he asked.

"The FBI will be here soon enough; I'll be okay."

When Lester left for the village, Marjorie went to her room and pulled a wooden keepsake box from her drawer. She brought it to the bed and fished for the letter Maynard had written after she ended their relationship. His words were as painful as the first time she had read them twenty-five years ago.

He promised to love her and give his life for her. Weeping uncontrollably, clutching the letter, Marjorie poured out her sadness. She emptied her sorrow until she fell asleep. The doorbell sounded. *It's Hannah Bates.* She hurried to the bathroom, combed her hair, washed her face, then ran downstairs.

Hannah was alone, and Marjorie invited her inside the house. They sat in the living room.

"How are you feeling?" Hannah asked.

"I'm shaken up, but I'll be alright."

"Mrs. Best, have you had any unusual interactions with a man lately?" Bates asked.

Marjorie hesitated. Stanley Hartman popped into her head, but she was uncomfortable pointing the finger at him. Although he made her uneasy, he appeared to be an unhappy, lonely, and harmless man.

"Not really," she said.

"The other night, when your husband thought Maynard Krantz may have been the person who assaulted you, you quickly came to his defense. How well did you know Mr. Krantz?"

Uneasy with the question, she stammered, unsure how much to share, and Hannah noticed. "Anything you tell me is completely confidential," she said.

"Maynard and I dated years ago, but I broke it off. He married another woman, yet he tried to reestablish a relationship with me several times over the years. I never let it happen."

"How recently had he tried?"

"Why is this important?" Marjorie asked.

"He saved you when you were in trouble on a deserted road, Mrs. Best. It's not a coincidence."

"Yesterday, I stopped by his shop while canvassing for donations. He gave me thirty dollars, and he wanted to talk. I cut him off, knowing his intentions. Later, when I walked home from the meeting, he stood outside Blake's Bar with a beer. I'm sure he saw me. He probably was drunk and followed me, wanting to continue our discussion."

Hannah wrote in her notebook, asking, "Have you noticed any men attracted to you recently? Any form of acknowledgment, no matter how slight."

"Is this necessary?"

"Yes, it is," Bates said.

"Oh, my lord, I can't believe I'm telling you these things. I've noticed a few men I don't know looking at me."

"How about the ones you know?"

"Oh, geez, let's see. I saw Stick Larson staring at me in the grocery store. So did Harry Michaels. Last week, Johnny Johns watched me with a smile from the moment I got out of my car until I walked inside the post office. In his eighties, Johnny does that to anyone without a penis."

"Anyone else?"

Marjorie crossed her arms and said, "I caught Reverend Dietrich staring at my breasts after church a few weeks ago. I can't believe I told you that. I turned my head toward him, noticed, and he turned away, red-faced. The poor man's wife is in Africa doing the Lord's work; he's probably as horny as a rabbit."

"Is that it?" Hannah asked.

"Isn't that enough? Yes, I believe that's it."

Hannah stood and handed her a card. "Please contact me if you think of anything else." Before leaving, Hannah asked if she felt safe at home alone.

"I have my husband's shotgun in the broom closet," Marjorie said. "If that son-of-a-bitch comes around here, he'll be pissing through his ass. Excuse me; I didn't mean to say that."

The FBI agent looked at her, smiled, and walked out.

Marjorie felt uncomfortable by describing insignificant sexual incidents. She felt strangely vulnerable. She calmed herself and called Julie.

"I'm so glad you called me back," Julie said. "I heard what happened; it's all over town. Are you okay?"

"I'm physically alright, but I can't stop thinking about Maynard. Everyone considered him a loser, but he saved my life and was always kind to me."

"I'm sorry about calling him a grump," Julie said. "I forgot the two of you were an item when you were young."

"That's okay. Maynard was grumpy. I may have contributed to his heartbreak."

"Are you scared about the guy who attacked you?" Julie asked.

"The gravity of the situation hasn't hit me yet. The notion someone tried to kill me will horrify me once I come to terms with it. I've done nothing to anyone."

"I can't believe someone is going around killing people," Julie said. "Everyone says it's a serial killer and might even be someone we know. Would you like company? I can stop by this afternoon."

"I feel like being alone today. Let's talk tomorrow."

When she hung up, Marjorie saw Lester's note to call Reverend Dietrich. Although she wasn't feeling up to it, she thought she should.

She was relieved Amy Chapman answered. "The Reverend is out for the day," she said.

"Oh, there's no need for him to call me back; I'm just returning his call. He wanted to know how I'm doing; please tell him I'm fine and will see him in church on Sunday."

"We are all so worried about you," Amy said. "And it's so awful what happened to poor Maynard. Do you think they'll get the guy?" Amy was a sweet woman in her sixties but a notorious busybody.

"I hope so," Marjorie said. She wanted to hang up and politely ended the conversation.

She went to the sofa. Covering herself with a blanket, she thought of Maynard and felt guilty. Lester didn't know she was grieving another man's loss. *He doesn't deserve this,* she thought. *I feel unfaithful.*

She imagined what her life might have been if she and Maynard had stayed together and had a family. Marjorie desperately wanted children but never conceived. She wanted to unload her guilty thoughts with someone, so she looked forward to Julie's visit.

CHAPTER NINE

Maddy

Maddy headed to Lester's Hardware Store to arrange for installing deadbolts on her house's doors. It was nearly noon, and Lester was just opening. The store usually opened at 8:00, and she wondered what was happening.

As she walked to the back, she noticed the typically composed man had dark circles under his eyes, and his hand trembled when he unlocked the register.

"Hi, Maddy," he said, avoiding eye contact.

"You don't look well, Lester," she said. "Are you okay?" He looked at her with tears in his eyes.

"No," he said, trying to contain his emotions. She saw his hands shake as he removed his glasses and wiped his eyes.

"I'm sorry," he said. "The most awful thing happened to Marjorie. Someone attacked her last night." Whitfield popped into Maddy's head.

"She was walking home from a meeting at the chapel when a man jumped her and tried to kill her," he said. "Thank God Maynard Krantz saw it happening and tried to save her. Marjorie ran home, but the guy cut Maynard's throat. He's dead."

Oh my God, he killed Maynard? Maynard Krantz was a vigorous man of significant size, and it was hard for Maddy to believe Whitfield overpowered him.

"The FBI believes it's the same guy who killed Abigail and the other girl," Lester said.

"I'm sorry, Lester. How is Marjorie holding up?"

"She's acting alright, but I don't think it's hit her yet."

"I'd like to visit her. Do you think she'd mind?"

"I think she'd like that," he said. "I didn't mean to unload my problems on you. How can I help you?"

"That's alright. I'd like to have deadbolts installed on all my doors."

"Are you concerned about that guy, too?" he asked.

"Yes, I am concerned," she said.

"I can have Stick Larson come to your place this afternoon."

"Here's a key," she said. "I'm heading to Albany to see Adam and will be home late."

When Maddy left the hardware store, she stopped and looked around before entering her vehicle. It was a cool summer day in the mountains; the air was crisp. She watched people walking the streets and thought of Maynard Krantz. *He was a good guy. I wonder how many more victims Whitfield will take. These people are fish in a barrel. Marjorie was lucky to survive. But if she's the woman who sent him into this killing frenzy, he won't stop until he kills her.*

She got in the Jeep and started on the three-hour drive to Albany. She was unsure of how to express herself with Adam, but her feelings were powerful.

The earlier days' events replayed in her mind as her thoughts wandered. She felt Whitfield closing in on her, and needed to talk with Adam before it was too late. *He needs to understand where I am on this.*

While lost in her thoughts, the rocket-like structures of New York's capital appeared in the distance. After worming her way through the city streets, Maddy arrived at Albany Medical Center. She parked, walked into the lobby, and gave her name to the woman behind the desk.

"I'd like to see Adam Forsyth," she said.

"Is he expecting you?"

"No, but he'll see me." The woman called a number and spoke in a low tone.

"Have a seat," she said. "He'll be down shortly."

Maddy sat, watching a few families leave as she waited. The elevator door opened, and her heartbeat picked up when Adam stepped out with a walker, his head still wrapped in white bandages. Walking over smiling, when he reached her, he pushed the walker aside, pulled her close, and wrapped his arms around her without saying a word. She melted into his embrace, and his warmth was like cuddling up into a soft blanket on a winter's night.

"Let's sit," he said. He grabbed the walker, and they moved to a place where they could be alone.

"Is everything okay?" he asked.

"We need to talk face-to-face. I couldn't talk to my father before he died, and I don't want the same to happen again with you." He spoke, but Maddy put her fingers to his lips and stopped him. "Listen to me," she said. "This is my time. I may not have much left." Adam sat back as though preparing to be jolted.

"We don't own the good in our lives," she said. "We want to hold on to it, make it ours, and possess it. It's like the first spring day after a long, cold winter. The birds make their nests, and flowers bloom. We want the moment to last."

"But spring passes, and before we know it, the leaves fall from the trees, and the flowers die. These years are not ours. We're only passing through."

"You'll always be a part of me," she said. "You've made a place in my heart every time you didn't interfere. It was as though you've always known I'll suffocate if I can't be myself. But our love is about to be tested."

"Aww, Maddy, how did we get here?" Adam said. "When we first met, I knew you were a relentlessly independent person. I was proud I could make you happy by letting you be who you were, but now that I'm so in love with you, I can't bear the thought of losing you."

"That's the test I'm talking about, Adam. It involves having faith in me and us. You can't be part of what's coming. It involves only me. Amos Whitfield has come to Berry Lake to kill me, and I must face him on my terms. Neither Hannah nor you can do it for me. The surest way to get me killed would be if you tried."

"Witnessing you go through this alone is the toughest thing I'll ever do," Adam said.

"I'm sorry for that," she said. "But if I'm going to survive this, I can't be trying to ease your fears. Do you understand?" Adam put his elbows on his knees, dropped his head in his hands, and nodded as he looked at the floor.

"I understand," he said.

"Thank you," she said. She reached over, held his head to her breast, and whispered, "I love you."

They sat back, holding hands in silence, and a sense of peace came over Maddy as the late afternoon sun shone through the lobby windows. She felt she had accomplished what she had come to do.

"I should get heading home," she said. Adam walked her to the front door, shuffling along with his walker. They hugged and shared a last look before parting ways.

"Goodbye, babe," she said. She carried his warmth with her as she entered her vehicle. Pulling out of the lot, she saw Adam standing outside the hospital door, leaning on his walker, and watching her leave.

•　　•　　•

It had only been weeks since she took the route back to Berry Lake from the hospital, but she didn't recognize her life now. The hills grew taller; the light grew dimmer, and soon she was in darkness. Passing through tiny hamlets and long stretches of mountain road, Adam was on her mind. *How close am I to losing him?* The thought shook her.

Maddy didn't understand the part of her that recoiled at being hemmed in. Yet, as much as she needed space to breathe, she needed someone to love, and Adam had fulfilled that need. She wondered if she was asking too much. The idea of choosing her independence over him caused her immense pain because she knew she'd set him free if it came to that.

Yet, living alone for the rest of her life was Maddy's deepest fear. At twelve, she developed anxiety after her father passed away. There was no one else for her, so she had to live with her grandmother, whom she hardly knew. Maddy couldn't let anyone near that lonely place within herself. It belonged only to her, and she put up impenetrable walls to protect it. She wondered if Adam might crash into that part of her someday, and the thought made her nauseous.

As she approached Berry Lake, she passed by where the roadblock had been; it felt like a year ago. She slowed as she entered the village. The lights in Lena's were still on, and she noticed Rose inside cleaning up, getting ready to close. She parked in front of the diner.

"Do you have time to talk?" she asked when she opened the door. It was just the two of them.

"Oh, deary, it's so good to see you," Rose said as she walked over and put her arms around her. "Let me lock the front door and dim the lights. Have a seat."

Rose's friendship had always been a warm spot in Maddy's life. Rose walked to the table with two cups of coffee and set them down. "It's decaf," she said.

"Has there been any news about Phoebe?" Maddy asked.

"Amy Chapman said she knows of someone who's seen her in the woods three times," Rose said.

"That's odd," Maddy said. Rose wondered why.

"Once is random, but three times suggests a search," Maddy said. "Phoebe has been coming around my place when I'm not around. I started leaving her food, and when I checked, it was gone." She shook her head. "I'm afraid for the girl because if Whitfield finds her, he'll kill her."

"I still can't comprehend Abigail raising her alone in that house all these years with no one knowing," Rose said.

"Oh, someone knew. Phoebe said her Aunt Betsy wanted her to attend school, but Abigail refused. They had a falling out, and Phoebe said it was why she ran away."

"Aunt Betsy?" Rose said. "I never knew of anyone around here named Betsy."

"Where is Abigail from?" Maddy asked.

"Lake Placid," Rose said.

"Was she ever engaged in the community?"

"I remember her attending church for a while. But when Reverend Crumb took over, she stopped going. He was the Reverend before Reverend Dietrich. Crumb was a fire-and-brimstone preacher who frequently mentioned hell. Abigail never came back."

Maddy peered into the darkness from the window. "Many pieces are missing," she said. She looked back at Rose. "Come on, let me give you a ride home."

After dropping Rose off at her apartment, she returned to her place. The Jeep crawled up the gravel road, and the house's silhouette was visible in the moonlight. She went inside and noticed lamplight in the kitchen. A set of keys lay on top of a note on the counter. It read: *Maddy, I installed deadbolts on the doors, including the outside basement door. Here are the keys. Stay safe, Maddy. Stick Larson.*

She smiled, thinking of the tall, skinny man who earned the name Stick by his long stick-like legs. *What a kind soul he is,* she thought.

Before going to her room, Maddy checked the newly installed locks and the windows, then placed her weapon on the nightstand beside her bed. Pleased with her discussion with Adam, she changed into nightclothes and crawled under a blanket. Yet the frightened child in the woods and Maynard Krantz's murder weighed heavily on her mind.

· · ·

The following morning, she slept late. The sun was over the mountains. Maddy sipped coffee on the deck, embraced the cooing of mourning doves, and basked in the comforting warmth of the sun as she contemplated her plans for the day.

Marjorie! I want to visit Marjorie. She felt a bond with the other person targeted by the killer. After showering and getting dressed, she headed for town, arrived at the Best home, and Marjorie opened up when she knocked.

"Hi, Maddy, come in. Lester mentioned you might stop by." Marjorie wore a housecoat and appeared pale and tired. "Sorry for my appearance," she said. "I haven't been feeling well." Walking to the kitchen, she asked her to excuse the mess and offered a glass of iced tea.

"Sure," Maddy said.

"I suppose you've heard about what happened," Marjorie said as she lay two glasses on the table and sat.

"Yes, Lester told me."

Maddy knew Marjorie less than her husband, but she always appeared friendly and outgoing. But that day, Marjorie looked traumatized.

"Do you know about the person who attacked you?" Maddy asked.

"Only what the FBI told me. They said he's a known serial killer that they've been tracking for years."

"His name is Amos Whitfield," Maddy said. Marjorie's eyes locked on her as she spoke. "What I'm going to tell you might horrify you, and unless you prefer I don't, I'll tell you everything. You have a right to know."

"I want to know," Marjorie said.

"Amos Whitfield moves into a community long before he kills. He's like a cancerous tumor spreading throughout the body, infecting one organ, then the next. He only attacks women and always takes at least one organ after he kills them. People think he was likely a trained surgeon." Marjorie sat back with folded arms, looking as if watching a horror flick.

"Are you sure you want me to continue?"

"Yes, please. I need to know what I'm dealing with."

"Whitfield has a quirk," Maddy said. "If he feels slighted by a woman for whom he has romantic feelings, he loses control and starts killing rapidly. It's called a killing frenzy. His ego is so hypersensitive that the woman may not realize she's rebuked him. I'm not saying you're that person, but you may be."

"Hannah Bates asked about men who appeared attracted to me," Marjorie said.

"Were you able to tell her about anyone with whom you've had a strange interaction?"

"I thought of Stanley Hartman, but I didn't tell her. I didn't want to get him in trouble."

"Hartman?" Maddy asked. She remembered seeing the name on the list of men on Hannah's desk.

"He opened the tailor shop on Main Street," Marjorie said.

"You should tell her about him so she can run a background check." Maddy didn't know Marjorie well but wanted to assess her inner strength and started asking questions.

"Did you grow up here?"

"Yes, my father had a farm outside of the village."

"Did you ever hunt?"

"All the time. I had three brothers, and my father let us take off school the first week of deer season to hunt with him. We filled up the freezer with venison every year." Maddy asked if she'd ever killed a deer, and Marjorie said several.

"Do you and Lester keep a weapon in the house?" she asked.

"I have Lester's shotgun in the broom closet." She nodded her head to the narrow door next to the pantry. "I'm so scared, Maddy. That man wants to kill me."

Maddy reached out and put her hand on Marjorie's. "He wants to kill me, too." Marjorie looked at her, confused. "He's been taunting me; he'll be coming after me soon, so we're in the same boat."

"Aren't you petrified?"

"I'm scared but not petrified. If I became petrified, I couldn't take action."

Marjorie asked if she had killed people.

"Yes, more than I'd care to admit."

"I wish I had your strength and courage. I don't know if I have what it takes to shoot a person."

"No need to worry about that. If the situation presents itself—and let's hope it won't—your instincts will kick in."

Marjorie thanked her. "You're the only person I know who's dealt with people like this Whitfield guy." As she stood to leave, Maddy said she was there if needed. "Thank you for coming to see me; I don't feel so alone anymore." She followed her to the door, and when Maddy turned to say goodbye, she threw her arms around her neck and then quickly let go.

"I'm sorry," she said. "I'm just so scared."

"That's okay," Maddy said. "Call me if you feel like talking."

CHAPTER TEN

Hannah

Hannah stepped into the command center as Allen Bowers frantically wrote on a yellow pad with a telephone to his ear.

"He's talking with the Franklin County Sheriff about a missing person," Sara whispered.

Allen hung up, finished his note, and looked at Hannah. "A woman named Elizabeth Beckman disappeared this morning in Lake Placid," Allen said. "She didn't show up for the fundraising event in Saranac Lake. The sheriff wanted to alert us. He said she's quite wealthy and owns several properties throughout the Adirondacks. They're checking her homes because sometimes she changes plans and visits her places. One is just outside of Berry Lake."

"We can check out the home in Berry Lake," Hannah said.

"They said they've got it covered," Allen said.

Hannah went to her desk to review the list of recent male residents. "What's the progress on the background checks?"

"About half done. So far, they're all clean."

"Agent Bates," a tech called out, holding a phone. "Sheriff Cerio from Franklin County is on the phone again and wants to speak with you."

"This is Dan Cerio, the Franklin County Sheriff. We just found Elizabeth Beckman's body in a park about a mile from her home. She looks like a Whitfield victim. How do you want to handle this?"

"Leave things as they are. I'm giving you to Agent Bowers. Please give him the directions to a heliport; we'll need to land two helicopters and bring our forensic team." Her stomach tightened as she gave the phone to Allen. "The son-of-a-bitch isn't letting any grass grow under his feet," she said. Lake Placid was sixty miles from Berry Lake, and Hannah realized Whitfield was working in a wider geographic range than she thought.

"Sara, contact law enforcement agencies within a hundred-mile radius. Request all outstanding missing person reports from the past three months and future cases." She turned to Allen. "Whitfield is picking up his killing pace, and I have a sinking feeling he's entering a frenzy. Is the list of upcoming social events available?"

"It's on your desk. The town fair is the largest gathering, and they're going ahead. The town council has already paid the vendors and won't cancel."

"Just great," she said. "It's like serving up a buffet for the guy." She remembered Ted Bundy used large public gatherings to steal away victims, and the town fair was perfect for Whitfield to do his thing.

"The helicopter is ready, Hannah," Sara said.

The agents and forensics team boarded two helicopters in the school parking lot. In the air, she got a call from her boss. "What information do we have on the Placid victim?" Harris asked.

"We're on our way to the scene now. I'll let you know what I find out," she said.

She arrived in Lake Placid, and a half dozen sheriff's cars waited to take the FBI unit to the scene. Hannah walked to an unmarked vehicle where a tall, dark-skinned man with curly white hair waited beside an open rear door and said, "I'm Dan Cerio."

"Hannah Bates," she said as she shook his hand.

She got in, and as they moved on a winding road with tall pines on each side, Cerio discussed Elizabeth Beckman. "She's a beloved person in the Placid community," he said. "Her family has made significant contributions to many good causes. There'll be an uproar when word gets out what's happened to her. She's considered an extremely warm-hearted woman."

"Do you know what time she left her house?" Hannah asked.

"She left at about nine this morning. She didn't arrive at a fundraising event, which was unusual because she was the sponsor. She's been raising money for a children's cancer wing at the local hospital; it was her pet project. We found the body about twelve-forty-five, just a little before I called you."

They arrived at the scene, and Beckman's Lincoln was barely visible in the tall grass at the rear of a small park. The place had picnic tables and a trash bin but no public toilets.

"Who uses this park?" Hannah asked.

"Hardly anyone since the county put in Cashman Community Center," he said. "Teens come here to drink." Hannah thought it was a perfect spot for a secret meeting.

An army of sheriff's vehicles surrounded the spot, and men and women milled around. Cerio led Hannah to the car, where the trunk was open, and when she stepped around, she saw a slender woman in her late sixties inside the enormous trunk with her knees up. A hole in her throat, wide enough to fit a fist, and a torn, bloodied white summer dress exposing her open thoracic cavity sent a chill through Hannah. Horror riddled the woman's face. Beckman's heart was missing, and someone had tied off the connected arteries with a blue string. The sight had all the markings of Amos Whitfield.

"It looks like someone stole her warm heart," Hannah said. Cerio nodded, grim-faced. She stepped back, allowing the forensics team to go ahead.

When Hannah learned Amos Whitfield was the perpetrator, she knew it was her most challenging assignment yet. But she didn't expect the frenzy. He'd killed four people in three weeks and tried to kill a fifth. She had little time to stop him before he claimed more victims. Hannah dispatched two agents to interview the residents at the Beckman home before getting on the helicopter back to the command center. She called Harris when she departed.

"Ben, it appears to have been Whitfield again. He's widening his net."

"You better get the missing persons reports from law enforcement in the area and check out any upcoming public gatherings," he said.

She didn't bother telling him she'd done both and said, "Got it."

The helicopter landed in the school parking lot. Hannah got out, walked inside, went to her desk, and sat. She took a pen and a notebook, drew five boxes on a sheet of paper, wrote victim names on top of each box, and started filling in murder details.

Box 1. Abigail Hicks — murdered. She met with her killer privately and must have had a prior relationship.

Box 2. Beverly Arnold — murdered. She did not know her killer. It appeared to be random. Someone may have followed her from Reynolds' home.

Box 3. Maynard Krantz — murdered trying to save Marjorie Best. Completely random.

Box 4. Marjorie Best survived an attack by a man wearing a ski mask. She likely knew the attacker.

Box 5. Elizabeth Beckman — murdered. She met her killer privately and must have had a prior relationship.

Hannah examined the boxes, then circled one and five. *Abigail Hicks and Elizabeth Beckman met their killer and must have had a relationship with him.*

"Agent Bates, we may have something," an agent called out. "It looks like Stanley Hartman, a local tailor new to the area, has changed his identity. We've had our people in D.C. look into every Stanley Hartman, and none can plausibly be the tailor. Our best guess is he purchased credentials required to register a vehicle in New York State and has been using the name for about a year."

"Okay," she said. "We'll have an agent visit him. We'll say we're interviewing all men new to the area. I don't want him to think we're focused only on him."

Sara held a slip of paper with the name David Preston as Hannah turned to her. "Sheriff Cerio called and said this man has worked for Mrs. Beckman, kept her schedule, and might be helpful."

"Where is Allen?" Hannah asked.

"He just left with the local sheriff to identify an abandoned car," Sara said.

"Okay, please get Preston on the phone for me."

Sara left her, and Hannah looked at the calendar, thinking of the fast-approaching town fair. *Shit, I can't believe these people are following through with that damn event.* Sara returned with a phone in her hand.

"It's David Preston."

Hannah grabbed the receiver. "Hello, Mr. Preston; this is Hannah Bates from the FBI. I have a few questions about Elizabeth Beckman's schedule, and we heard you were the person to ask."

"Yes, I kept her schedule," he said, "but before you begin, understand that she was very secretive about what she did. She'd make appointments, and I'd put them on the calendar, but then she wouldn't go. Sometimes, she'd turn up somewhere unscheduled. It was very frustrating."

"Do you know who she left her house with this morning?"

"Your agents just asked me the same question. To the best of my knowledge, she left alone."

"Do you remember scheduling Abigail Hicks, or she may have gone by the name Abigail Newton?"

"No, I don't recall either of those names," he said.

"Can you fax the schedule to us, Mr. Preston?" She handed the phone to Sara. Like airplanes backed up over an airport after a storm, situations requiring Hannah's attention, one after the next, waited.

"Hannah, we have Allen on the line," another of the techs said.

"Put it over to my desk." Her head felt as though it would burst. She picked up the phone and asked Allen what he had.

"Someone reported an abandoned 1988 Ford Galaxy at Eddy's Pond. The tire tracks match those we found at the Beverly Arnold murder scene. Two weeks ago, someone stole the car from the parking lot behind Blake's Bar."

"That's what I thought," she said. "Scrub it for prints, but I doubt you'll find anything."

Frustrated, she looked around for Larry from forensics. "Has anyone seen Simmons?" she shouted. "I need the goddamn forensics report from the murder scene in Lake Placid." She gazed around, and everyone was looking at her. Hannah knew it was an absolute no-no for someone in her position to lose control. She turned to Sara and whispered that she was taking a walk.

She went to a park, sat on a bench, and gazed at the water. *Get a hold of yourself, Hannah.* She watched a sailboat glide in the distance, took deep breaths, and tried to calm herself. Things were happening fast, and Whitfield was two steps ahead of her. *The bastard is killing more rapidly than we can investigate.* She closed her eyes and thought of Anthony and Charles, breathing deeply until the tension in her body melted away. Hannah returned to the command center, determined to find a crack in the seemingly impenetrable mystery.

Allen had returned, and she felt relieved. He was holding a stack of faxed papers, and she asked what they were. "It's Elizabeth Beckman's schedule. Sara just handed it to me." The faxed pages of the scheduling book had notes, appointments, and scratched-out appointments. He laid them on the table, and the two examined how Elizabeth Beckman spent her days.

"Look," Allen said. "There's a star every other Tuesday, but no name. It looks like a standing appointment, the kind you always remember."

"And the kind you don't want anyone else to know about," Hannah added.

CHAPTER ELEVEN

Marjorie

Marjorie walked into the kitchen as Lester read the newspaper at the table. He rested it on his lap when he saw her.

"How are you feeling this morning?" he asked.

"I'm getting back to being myself. I've hated feeling so anxious."

"Doc Peters said it would take time, Marj,"

"I know; I'm just getting impatient."

"Do you have anything planned for today?" he asked.

"Let's see. I might shower and get dressed. Then I planned to watch the grass grow before taking a nap."

"It can't be that bad," he said.

"You try being stuck in this house, too afraid to walk outside. It's not a lot of fun."

He reached over, put his hand on hers, and said he'd try to be home early. "I need to get moving," he said. He left for work, and Marjorie sat at the kitchen table, sipping tea. She pulled the Albany newspaper to her, but nothing grabbed her interest. She started upstairs to shower when the phone rang.

"Hi, Marj, it's Julie. Feel like company today?"

"You don't even know," she said. "Yes, I'd love some. All this is just sinking in. Poor Lester tries to be comforting but has such a hard time."

"I'll be over about noon and bring lunch," Julie said.

Marjorie hung up, thinking she didn't understand why she felt like she did. *This is not me.* She went upstairs, showered, dressed, and looked forward to visiting with Julie. *I'm too preoccupied with my thoughts.* She returned and anxiously waited, occasionally peeking out the front door window. Finally, she heard a knock, and Julie stood at the door holding a grocery bag.

"Dear Lord, it's so good to see you," Marjorie said as she put her arms around Julie. "Let me take this," she said, grabbing the bag and heading to the kitchen.

She lifted out corned beef sandwiches, chicken soup, and homemade chocolate cake when she brought it to the counter. "My, what a peach you are," she said.

The two friends prepared the meal, sat, and started eating.

"They held Abigail's funeral services yesterday," Julie said.

"Oh, dear, I completely forgot."

"No one expected you to be there after what happened to you."

"I'm sure it was wonderfully done," Marjorie said.

"The ceremony and headstone were quite beautiful. Reverend Dietrich did an amazing job of putting everything together. He even mentioned you in his sermon and asked everyone to pray for you." Marjorie expressed her regret for not being present.

"I feel like all that has happened has steamrolled me, and I can't wrap my head around someone trying to kill me. I wonder if it was random or because of something I've done."

"Oh, Marjorie, what could you have possibly done to warrant being killed?"

"I know, but somewhere in this town, there's a deranged person with a distorted view of reality. Maybe I did something disturbing to him."

"It had to be random," Julie said. "Look at that girl from Tupper Lake; she was just passing through here. It had to be random, Marjorie."

"It makes me feel better thinking that, otherwise, the guy might return for me." She didn't share the possibility the killer was in a killing frenzy and fixated on her, as Maddy Reynolds had pointed out. She kept pushing that notion out of her mind.

"It also sounds like you're struggling with the loss of Maynard," Julie said.

"Yes, I am. No one knew how close we'd become in high school. I kept our relationship very secret because my father hated him. He thought he'd become a bum. We'd grown to be very close; I truly loved Maynard."

She put her sandwich on her plate and folded her hands. "I've never shared this with a soul, but my mother told me my father hated him because he reminded him of himself. The more my father distrusted me, the more I wanted to be with Maynard. The loft in his father's barn became a regular stop after school. Then we started making love."

"I'll never forget the day I thought I was pregnant and was so scared I broke it off. I couldn't imagine what my father would have done. Thank goodness it was a false alarm. Maynard tried hard to get me back, but I couldn't. I wonder if I did the right thing." Julie reached over and took her hand.

"Everyone has regrets and doubts about decisions they made when they were young."

"I wanted kids so badly," Marjorie said. "Lester and I…well, it just never happened. Romance was never his strong suit. I wonder if it would have been different with Maynard," she said as she picked up her sandwich and started eating again.

After a few moments, she said, "I never realized how awful it feels to be paralyzed by fear. Maddy Reynolds stopped by to see me, and we talked about the difference between being petrified and being scared. I asked if she felt petrified when faced with a potential killer. She said she felt scared, not petrified. She said if something petrified her, she wouldn't be able to take action to protect herself."

"It's hard to believe we have someone like her living in our town," Julie said. "I don't know where she gets her courage."

"Just having Maddy nearby makes me feel safe," Marjorie said.

"What will you do now?"

"I'm going to have to push myself. I'll let myself stay home and be a baby for a few more days, but I'm attending church on Sunday. Fear will not run my life."

"We can sit together," Julie said.

Marjorie followed her out as she got up to leave, and when she stepped into the sunshine, she couldn't believe how uneasy she felt. *My mind is more affected by that incident than I realized,* she thought.

Saturday, the church services on Sunday were on her mind. That night in bed, she was restless, and Sunday morning, she awoke tired, with her mind foggy. She forced herself to get dressed for church.

"I'm leaving," she said to Lester.

"Are you sure about doing this? I can drive you."

"No, I want to walk. I've got to face these fears, eventually." She stepped outside, and tension, like electricity, ran through her veins. She approached the spot where the attack occurred, and her heart pounded. Pushing on, she struggled to catch her breath. By the time she entered the church, she was sweating.

"Over here," she heard Julie say, waving her to a pew. She walked over and sat beside her. The church was filling up with smiling faces, and the soft colors of its oak walls and ceilings gave her a warm feeling.

"Are you alright?" Julie asked.

"My God, I'm a nervous wreck," Marjorie said. She wiped her head with a tissue as the organ played *How Great Thou Art*. She picked up a hymnal, started singing, and her heartbeat slowed. When the reverend went to the pulpit to speak, she listened to every word.

"Everyone has dark nights," he said with a powerful, resonating sense of purpose. "We think we're alone and cringe in our darkness, but God is with us. He knows us better than we know ourselves. Our greatest enemy is doubt, so we must doubt our doubts and remain steadfast by trusting in one another. If we do this, we'll have nothing to fear." Marjorie felt as though he was talking directly to her.

When Dietrich finished and they sang the final hymn, Marjorie sighed, looked at Julie, and smiled. "I feel so much better." The reverend walked over when the service ended and asked how she was doing. "I'm hanging in there," she said.

"Well, it's wonderful seeing you here," he said as he walked her out into the sunshine. They stopped, and Julie walked ahead.

"Do you think you'll start attending Wednesday's healing prayer group?" he asked.

"What's it all about?" she asked.

"We pray and perform the laying on of hands. It's quite wonderful."

"Reverend, please don't take offense, but I'm uncomfortable with that type of prayer group." He nodded, smiled, and put out his hand.

"Well, that's okay. We'll be here if you change your mind. Have a blessed day," he said. She shook his hand and walked to where Julie waited, talking to Ernie Bajorek.

"Hi, Marjorie," Ernie said when she walked over.

"Hello," she said.

"I was just telling Julie how relieved I am you survived that attack. It must have been traumatic. And it's hard to believe that Maynard Krantz died like that."

"Thank you."

"I see my wife over by the car waiting for me," he said. "I better go, but I'm glad to see you here today."

"He's not such a bad person," Julie said when Ernie walked away. "He seemed genuinely concerned for you. We probably should have let him walk us home that night."

"Maybe," Marjorie said. "But I'm uneasy about trusting any man I don't know right now."

Julie said she understood. "So, are you glad you came today?"

"Socializing gets me out of my mind. All I've been doing is sitting around worrying."

They reached Julie's house and stopped. "Déjà vu," Marjorie said, thinking of a few nights earlier when she walked Julie to her house. Her insides were tightening.

"Do you want me to walk you home?" Julie asked.

"It's amazing, but I can feel my heart pounding. I'll pass; I need to keep going."

For the rest of the way home, everything moved in slow motion. She carefully navigated to where the attack took place, pondering Maynard's demise. A torrent of sadness unexpectedly rose from her gut, filling her eyes with tears. She kept walking and entered her house. Lester sat with a beer in his hand, watching a baseball game on television. She ran to her room, fell onto the bed, and wept asleep.

It was midafternoon when she awoke. She felt groggy, and it took a moment to remember it wasn't morning. Lester was asleep in a chair with the television on when she walked downstairs. With an urge to cook, she went to the kitchen, pulled out a beef roast, and started preparing a meal. Her mind finally felt at peace.

"What smells so good?" Lester asked when he stepped into the kitchen.

"I finally cooked that roast."

"Now it feels like things are returning to normal," he said. "So, how was church today?"

"Wonderful. Leaving the house made me uneasy, but talking with people felt great. Lester, can you not watch television tonight? Let's do something different; let's play cards."

"Okay, sounds like fun."

After dinner, Lester assisted with the kitchen cleanup. They unfolded a card table and played pinochle.

"Let's play one more," Lester said after each of them won a game. "This is for the championship."

Marjorie shuffled the deck and dealt out the cards. "Read them and weep," she said when she finished dealing. Forty-five minutes later, she yelled, "I won!"

Lester sat back in his chair and said, "I'm exhausted, but I had fun." That night in bed, before they slept, he told her he loved her. Hearing his words made her feel closer to her husband than she had in years.

While making tea downstairs the next day, she heard a cardinal singing outside and glanced out the window. "Where are you, pretty cardinal?" she said before she sat with her tea. The front screen door appeared ajar, and she got up, opened the wooden door to close it, and noticed a shoe box wrapped with brown paper on the threshold.

Bringing it to the kitchen table, she noticed a tag that said, *For Marjorie.* Tearing open the brown paper, she lifted the lid and pulled out a soft, squishy item wrapped in tissue paper. Unraveling the tissue, her eyes bugged out as she bellowed a high-pitched scream. Blood oozed from the tubular stems of an object squeezed into a plastic bag. "It's a human heart!" she screamed. A note read: *You need this warm heart; yours is cold.*

Screaming and holding her head, Marjorie couldn't avert her gaze from the bloody object. She heard herself shrieking and felt detached from her body. Turning to hold on to the sink, she steadied herself and vomited.

Lester rushed into the kitchen. "What is it?" he said as he ran to his wife.

She pointed to the kitchen table and screamed, "It's a heart!" Lester stiffened as he and his wife clung to each other, edging away from the repulsive-looking human organ on the table.

Lester reached for the phone in the living room and the FBI agent's card in the end table drawer. He dialed and asked for Bates. "This is Lester Best," he said. "There's a human heart on my kitchen table."

CHAPTER TWELVE

Hannah

Allen drove to Lester and Marjorie Best's house as Hannah stared out the passenger-side window with folded arms. Watching the pine trees passing by, her mind ran full throttle. "Whitfield is winning," she said. "He's a step ahead of us at every turn. That heart belongs to Elizabeth Beckman."

She turned to Allen. "Marjorie Best must be the woman who made Whitfield go on a killing spree. She must have inflicted an emotional wound on him somehow. If we don't get to him first, he won't stop until he kills her."

Marjorie sat on the sofa, holding her head and staring at the floor when they arrived at the house. Hannah sat beside her while the other agents went to the kitchen with Lesser.

"Are you able to talk?" she asked.

"Yes," Marjorie said.

"This must have been a terrible shock."

"It was."

"Last time I asked about the men attracted to you, you gave me examples. Think about it again. Think of someone you've had a peculiar exchange with. It may seem insignificant, but it may not have been to that person."

"Stanley Hartman," Marjorie blurted out. "I had a strange interaction with him."

"What happened?"

"I asked him for a donation, and he seemed offended. He begrudgingly gave me a dollar and walked away. I made a snide comment, and he heard it and glared at me."

"Why didn't you mention this before?"

"I wasn't sure, so I said nothing. The guy looks lonely, and I didn't want to make his life worse than it already was."

A man with a black box came from the kitchen. *It's the heart*, Hannah thought. Lester and the others followed. Hannah turned back to Marjorie.

"We have a social worker available to talk to who is very understanding. Her name is Angela. Would you like to speak with her?"

"No, my husband has asked Doctor Peters, our family physician, to come by later to give me something to calm down."

Hannah made a note to check out the doctor. "Do you have questions for me?" she asked.

"Just one. Whose heart is it?"

"We think it belonged to a woman from Lake Placid," Hannah said. "Her name was Elizabeth Beckman. We'll help you through this, Marjorie, but you must work with us. We'll place a unit in front of your house and need your permission to listen in on your phone calls. Do you approve?"

"Yes," she said.

"We'll stay in close touch; you do the same," Hannah said.

Hannah went with Allen to the car, and she drove. "When is the interview with Hartman?"

"Agent Owens should be at his home now."

"We need to find a reason to hold the guy," she said. "Get Owens on the phone."

Allen took a cell phone from his pocket and dialed. "Agent Owens, Hannah Bates would like to speak with you," he said, then handed Hannah the phone.

"Have you started interviewing Hartman yet?" she asked.

"No, it looks like he's absconded. We knocked, but there was no answer, and the landlord said he hastily packed his car, paid the rent in cash, and took off."

"Damn it," she said. "Stay there. Make sure no one enters. We'll be sending the forensics team over." She handed the phone back to Allen. "Alert law enforcement in the region that Stanley Hartman is a suspect in several murders."

"Will do."

When she arrived, Hannah thought the three-story wooden building was perfect for Whitfield to blend. The smells of dust and old wood permeated the stairway as they walked up to the second floor. Agent Owens stood in the hall in front of Hartman's apartment, and as Hannah and Allen approached, he stepped aside. She asked if Larry Simmons had arrived, and Owens said he had. She and Allen entered cautiously, avoiding contamination, and waited near the entry for Simmons to emerge from another room.

"What have you found?" she asked.

"A lot of porn, but no body parts."

A voice called out, "I've got something." One of Larry's team brought a shoe box and handed it to her boss. With his hand in a rubber glove, Larry carefully picked up a few photos of women pulling up their underpants as they stood up from a toilet.

Hannah snapped around to Owens. "What time did Hartman leave here?"

"According to the landlord, about eleven-fifteen," he said. She looked at her watch.

"That was forty-five minutes ago. I want roadblocks on every road connected to Berry Lake in an eighty-mile radius," she said. "Allen, call the command center and have them get right on it. They are to use local law enforcement, state police, and sheriffs. The roadblocks should be in place within thirty minutes. Send his description and the details of his Subaru, warn them that the guy might be a deadly serial killer, and they are to take all precautions. We'll head the son-of-a-bitch off."

Larry Simmons was waiting when she finally returned to the command center after meeting with the sheriff. "Look at this," he said. Hannah watched him lift the lid off the shoe box. "Beneath the photos of women in the bathroom, we found these in tissue paper." Lifting the tissue-covered stack and laying them on the table, he pulled out a photo of Abigail Hicks leaving the post office and entering her car. Two pictures of Marjorie Best followed. "He photographed the Best woman on the same afternoon," he said. The last photo showed Elizabeth Beckman entering a thrift shop.

"He used a Minolta TC-1 to take these. It's a super-small, twenty-eight-millimeter camera that can easily fit inside a man's pant pocket. Unfortunately, he developed them, so we can't track him that way."

Hannah leaned her hands on the table, pondering the photographs.

"Thanks, Larry," she said. He left, but she stayed, contemplating the new information. Allen came over and asked for any updates. She slid over the photos.

"It looks like Hartman's our man," he said.

"Maybe," Hannah said.

It was approaching 1:00, and Hannah felt the tension of each passing moment. "It must happen in the next hour if Hartman is to be apprehended." The phone rang, and Allen answered. She hoped it was from a roadblock, but he signaled it was her boss and handed over the receiver.

"Hi, Ben."

"Any bites?" he asked, sounding anxious.

"Not so far. We should know within the hour."

"Do we have Hartman's true identity yet?"

"We're working on it."

"Let's not blow this, Hannah. If he escapes our net, God knows when he'll show up again, and we'll have another bite at the apple." Hannah didn't respond. There was an uncomfortable silence before he said, "Keep me posted."

The minutes ticked away, and finally, at 4:00, she realized it was too late; Hartman had evaded the net. She turned to Allen. "Bring down the roadblocks."

CHAPTER THIRTEEN

Frank Zepatello (Zep)

It was 8:15 AM, and Zep sat at his desk reading a fax from the FBI command center in Berry Lake. As steam floated from a Styrofoam cup, he sipped his coffee as he hit the intercom button. "Please find Al and Bud and have them come to my office." The two senior detectives entered, sharing verbal jabs over the upcoming Yankee and Red Sox game, and sat across from their boss.

"Where are we with Zerwillager?" he asked.

"Today is day three since she disappeared," Al said. "I checked with the parents this morning, and still no word."

"We got a fax from the command center in Berry Lake," Zep said. "They believe Amos Whitfield to be the perpetrator, possibly working over a broad region. They want information on any unresolved missing persons reported over the past four months. Run the Zerwillager details by me again."

"The girl's name is Sherry Zerwillager," Al said. "She's eighteen. She set off from Utica on Sunday afternoon to join friends in Saratoga. They spent time in the town, ate at a burger joint, and were at the Saratoga Performing Arts Center for the Sting concert by seven. She remained with the group until about midnight, when they split up. That was the last time anyone saw her. We got a call the next morning from her father, worried because she hadn't come home."

Zep leaned back in his chair and crossed his arms. "I want you guys all over this. I need to report it to Hannah Bates, but I'm not waiting for them to investigate. Let's get on it." He pondered his talk with Maddy as his right and left arms exited the room. *Fucking Whitfield is in a killing frenzy—Son-of-a-bitch.* He picked up the phone, dialed the command center number on the fax, and asked for Bates.

"Tell her it's Captain Frank Zepatello from the Oneida County Sheriff's."

"Hi, Zep, it's Hannah," she said when she came to the phone.

"Hannah, we've got a missing person, three days old. Her name is Sherry Zerwillager. She's from Utica, is eighteen, and was last seen at the Sting concert at SPAC in Saratoga Sunday night. Our guys are on it. I'll have more background later. It sounds like shit's hitting the fan up there."

"Yeah, Whitfield is entirely out of control. He's been killing people like they're going out of style."

"I talked with Maddy the other day," Zep said. "She told me about a girl who might identify Whitfield. Any luck on finding the kid?"

"No, he's either gotten to her already, and she's dead in the woods, or she's hiding somewhere."

"Zep, this is off the record. I believe Whitfield is communicating with Maddy. If he is, it's because he's come here to kill her. I don't expect you to tell me if she's shared this with you, but I hope you'll try to talk her out of going after him alone. Maddy is out of the bad guy business. She may not survive a confrontation with Amos Whitfield."

Zep didn't say it, but he'd never bet against Maddy Reynolds. He'd seen many tough men, but none had Maddy's skill of exploiting a person's weaknesses.

"She's always been headstrong," he said. "If what you're saying is true, I wouldn't be able to talk her out of it. Hopefully, the FBI locates Whitfield before it comes to that."

When they hung up, he thought of Maddy's circumstance. He wouldn't betray her trust and wished he could help somehow. After visiting one of his detectives in the hospital during lunch, Al was waiting in his office when he returned.

"How's Henry?" Al asked.

"He's alright. His pride is hurting worse than his wound. What's the situation with Zerwillager?"

"Bud's in Albany interviewing the girl's friends who were with her that night," Al said. "They were all freshmen at Siena College. I interviewed her family today and a few teachers at her alma mater, Notre Dame High School." Al laid a photo of the girl on the table. "This is her high school picture."

"Shit, she looks like my daughter," Zep said.

Al said the girl was driving a 1993 White Honda Civic. "We have the description out to law enforcement throughout the state. Sherry seems like a clean-cut kid. She's had no trouble with the law. She didn't even have a boyfriend until she started at Siena. He's touring Europe this summer with his parents, so he's out of the picture. The girl is on the cheerleading squad, runs track, and is a big deal in the church choir. She's your typical all-American teenager."

"Okay," Zep said. "Let's wait for Bud's input. Then you can compile a report for Bates."

Al got up and stopped at the door. "Is Maddy okay?"

Zep shook his head. "She thinks the killer is taunting her."

"How much shit does Maddy have to endure?" Al said. Zep didn't mention Whitfield had left her a kidney. He just shook his head and said he knew how he felt. When Bud returned from Albany around 4:00, the three detectives regrouped in Zep's office.

"Sherry's friends said she entered her car at twelve-twenty-five AM," Bud said. "They said she was an excellent driver who wouldn't get lost and wouldn't take off without notifying someone."

Bud added something else when Zep's phone rang. He picked up, listened, and said, "Make sure no one gets near the vehicle; we're on our way."

"That was the Utica police," he said as he placed down the phone. "They found the Civic in the Jefferson Elementary School parking lot. It's three blocks away from Zerwillager's house. Let's go." The men jumped into an unmarked car, and Bud drove. Al sat in the back, and Zep rode shotgun.

"Remember what Cupid did to those girls?" Zep said. "If this is Amos Whitfield's work, it will be worse." They pulled up to a school parking lot, and Zep saw a lonely white Honda Civic parked in a corner. A half dozen Utica Police units blocked the entrances. Bud pulled over, and they got out.

Captain Jordan of the Utica PD led the three sheriffs to the vehicle. Jordan said no one had been near the car. With each step, Zep felt his stomach tighten. He'd been doing police work a long time and had developed a sixth sense about bad situations. The lone Civic in the school parking lot, nestled near the building, screamed of bad.

They approached the car, stopped, and put on rubber gloves. Bud and Al opened the front and back doors; there was nothing. Al pulled the trunk release, and the four men froze. A young woman lay naked, with her throat opened wide, her eyes bugging out of their sockets, and her insides exposed from her pelvis to her sternum. The gaping hole where her reproductive organs were supposed to be was too much. Bud vomited, Al, crossed himself, and Jordan walked away with his eyes covered. Zep stood, staring at the body, remembering when he found a group of disemboweled comrades basking in the sweltering Vietnam sun. Like that day, he forced himself to remember the scene.

"Touch nothing," he said. "The FBI will handle this." He asked Jordan to keep his men there until he contacted Hannah Bates. The three sheriffs drove back to headquarters.

"I can't believe Maddy is dealing with this guy," Al said.

"What are you talking about?" Bud asked.

"Whitfield is communicating with her. Maddy thinks he wants to take her down."

The men had watched Maddy suffer under Cupid's torment until she ended his life. Bud shook his head. "The world is a fucked up and an unfair place," he said.

Bud and Al headed home when they returned to headquarters, and Zep went to his office to call Bates. "Hannah, Whitfield killed Sherry Zerwillager."

CHAPTER FOURTEEN

Maddy

The phone rang, Maddy answered, and her daughter sounded panicked.

"Mom, I just read about several homicides in Berry Lake. What's going on?"

Amber's excessive worrying over her mother's safety usually turned into blaming Maddy, which put Maddy on the defensive.

"The FBI thinks it's the work of Amos Whitfield," she said.

"Come to San Diego and stay with Todd and me. The twins would be so excited."

"I can't be far away from Adam while he's recovering."

Maddy had too much to handle in Berry Lake to engage in her daughter's hysteria.

"Why keep this from me until now?" Amber said, sounding annoyed.

"I didn't want to alarm you."

"How am I supposed to know if you're okay if you don't communicate with me? You are constantly distancing yourself."

"I'm sorry," Maddy said. "Maybe I should have made you aware, but you don't make sharing difficult situations easy."

"I just don't understand why you persist in putting yourself in harm's way," Amber said. "You've always done this."

"I don't do it intentionally, Amber. There's nothing I can do about it."

Amber snapped, "Suit yourself, Mom, but one of these days, your luck is going to run out, and you're going to get yourself killed. I have to go," she said, whimpering as she slammed the phone.

Damn it, maybe I should call her back, Maddy thought. For years, she blamed herself for Amber's struggles with anxiety.

Maddy remembered being concerned for her daughter when she first took the detective job. She thought the job might infringe on the time they were able to spend together. She couldn't have imagined the actual trauma they had to endure. Amber was only twelve when Cupid tormented them with threatening phone calls at home and even left a dead kitten on their front porch. Then he tried to kill Maddy, but the shotgun blast meant for her killed her friend instead.

Understanding the reasons for her daughter's hyper vigilance didn't stop it; it had gone on for years. Pacing around, trying to figure out what to do, she realized there was nothing. She didn't tell her she was in the crosshairs of a pathological killer. *I have to let it go.* She dressed before leaving to see Hannah, hoping to learn more about Phoebe.

Stepping into the command center, she realized she had made a mistake. The place was buzzing. The forensics team rushed past her to the parking lot, hopped in a van, and sped off while Hannah instructed half a dozen agents at her desk.

Hannah looked up, made eye contact, and motioned for her to come closer. As the agents cleared out, Maddy approached. "It looks like you have another situation," she said.

"We do, and it's right in your old stomping grounds," Hannah said. "Want to take a ride?"

"Sure; where are we going?"

"Utica. I figured you'd be coming around wanting an update on what's happening; we can catch up." They set out in Hannah's vehicle and had a moment alone to talk.

"What's the status of Phoebe?" Maddy asked.

"Nothing new." Sitting back in her seat, Maddy looked at the road ahead, thinking of the unusual freckle-faced redhead. The last time she'd left food, the girl hadn't taken it, and she wondered if she was still alive.

"Phoebe has been incredibly resourceful despite her sheltered life," Maddy said. "She must be highly intelligent. I wonder how long she can keep it up."

Hannah sighed. "I know. I feel like she's living on borrowed time, and if we don't get to her soon, her luck will run out." Maddy thought how unique the child was, and the notion of Whitfield trying to kill the girl deepened her hatred for the serial killer.

"What's happening in Utica?" she inquired.

"An eighteen-year-old girl named Sherry Zerwillager might be Whitfield's latest victim. Look at the preliminary report." Hannah handed over a folder. "That's the information gathered by your sheriff friends."

As she read, her stomach churned. "My God, he took all of her reproductive organs?" She slapped the folder closed and felt warmth around her neck as she clenched her fists. "How is it that forensics can't gather evidence on this person despite our advanced technology? It's 1996, for God's sake."

"I know. I've been thinking about that, too. The guy's a pro. He never leaves DNA or hair follicles—nothing. He probably gowns up before he does his thing."

"When I researched Whitfield, they believed he might be a surgeon," Maddy said.

"That's still the thinking," Hannah said. "The incisions on his victims are out of the medical books."

"I assume the FBI has looked into the enrollment databases of medical colleges and universities," Maddy said.

"We are culling through lots of data, but nothing yet." After several minutes of silence, Hannah said, "Maddy, there's something I must ask you."

Shit, here it comes, Maddy thought as she looked at her.

"Has Whitfield communicated with you?"

Maddy turned her eyes and looked straight ahead. "Why are you asking me that?"

"I've been trying to figure out why on earth he's come to Berry Lake when in the past he's moved into densely populated areas. He had to have followed Beverly Arnold from your house before he killed her, which means he'd been driving around near your place. There is nothing around your home. Just miles of roads, mountains, and woods. Whitfield might have an interest in the famous detective, Maddy Reynolds."

"Yes," Maddy finally said. "He's called me and left taunting messages. But I must tell you, Hannah, I won't allow the FBI to take control of my situation, including tapping my phone."

"You realize that means he may have come to Berry Lake to kill you, don't you?"

"I am keenly aware of that possibility," Maddy said.

"Why not allow us to place a unit near your place?"

"No, Hannah, that won't stop him, and you know it."

"You're doing it again," Hannah said. "You're going it alone. Why are you so stubborn about letting someone help you?"

"I don't entirely understand that about myself. It has something to do with not wanting to relinquish control, and it's caused me a lot of grief among my family and friends."

"If you genuinely care about your loved ones, why not prioritize them over your obsession with independence?" Hannah said.

"How long have you and I been having this discussion, Hannah? Fifteen years? Eighteen years? I'm not about to change how I am, nor are you. So why don't we stop butting heads and respect one another's positions? We might even become friends."

Hannah turned her head toward Maddy, looking sad. "I'd hate to lose a friend if there's something I can do to stop it."

"So, you're a lot like me," Maddy said. "You crave control as well."

"I suppose you're right." The women exchanged smiles.

They entered the city of Utica, and Hannah reached for a paper with directions. Maddy asked where they were going, and when she said Jefferson Elementary School, she started directing her. "That's where my daughter went to school."

Hannah pulled over a half block away from sheriff's cruisers and unmarked FBI and detective vehicles on the street. Only the white Honda Civic, the Oneida County Medical Examiner van, and the FBI's forensics van were in the parking lot. A cadre of men and women in suits stood waiting as the technicians huddled near the Civic's trunk. When Hannah and Maddy walked across the open space, Zep, Al Ramirez, and Bud Renshaw stepped out from among the crowd and met them halfway.

"Maddy," Zep said, opening his arms as she fell into them. Being held by someone she knew understood her and who she completely trusted felt like she was coming home after a long trip. Al and Bud stood nearby, waiting.

She looked at them and said, "Hey, guys." Bud said hey, and Al put his hand on her shoulder.

"The body's over here," Zep said, turning to Hannah. They walked to the Civic. With a disgusted look, Hannah said Whitfield was perfecting his surgical skills. Maddy thought of Beverly Arnold as she gazed at the desecrated body.

"Have you found anything else?" Hannah asked.

Zep, Al, and Bud exchanged glances. Zep pulled a plastic baggie from his suit pocket, handed it to her, and said, "Just this. We found it in the girl's pocket." It was a paper with typed words. "These lyrics are from a concert song. Sting wrote *Murder by Numbers*."

Hannah read the lyrics aloud. It referred to slipping a tablet into someone's coffee to avoid an awful mess before killing the person. She shouted, "Shit, the son-of-a-bitch drugged the girl." She turned to Allen Bowers and handed him the bag with the note. "Tell the toxicology people to be on the lookout for date-rape-type drugs."

"Here come the wigs," Bud said. Maddy remembered how Bud truncated words wherever possible, and 'wigs' was short for 'bigwigs.'

Everyone watched as the mayor and the new Utica Police Chief, Steven Moss, walked to them. Zep introduced everyone.

He got to Maddy, and Moss said he'd heard good things about her. "The community thinks highly of Maddy Reynolds." The mayor, disinterested in the chit-chat, asked where the body was.

"This way." Zep gestured to the car. The mayor's face twisted in disgust as he glanced at the trunk. Moss asked who'd be telling the parents.

"Me," Zep said. The wigs walked away, and Maddy gazed at Zep, knowing how difficult it was to tell a mother and father of their murdered child. He turned to her. "I'll stay in touch, Maddy."

•　　•　　•

Hannah and Maddy started on the ride back to Berry Lake.

"I think Whitfield is in a killing frenzy," Hannah said. Maddy asked if she knew the woman who triggered him. "We think it's Marjorie Best. You probably haven't heard, but he left the heart of a woman he killed in Lake Placid at her home. We're pretty sure Marjorie is the person."

"Who's the woman in Placid?"

"Elizabeth Beckman," Hannah said.

I'm living out a nightmare with no ending, Maddy thought. "Whitfield has Berry Lake tied into a knot," she said.

"I know. I feel like we're spinning our wheels."

They reached a long stretch of road with no houses or lights. It was dark, and there was silence until Hannah's cell phone rang. She listened before requesting to receive updates. "We may have gotten a break," she said. "Our people identified a man named Ernie Bajorek in a video from the Sting concert. Our database has him living outside of Berry Lake, and he has two priors related to identity theft."

"I know who he is," Maddy said. "He's married, seems well off, and they say he used to work on Wall Street."

"We'll be digging into his background. At least we now have two suspects." Maddy asked who the other suspect was. "It's a guy named Stanley Hartman."

"Hartman? He's the tailor, right?"

"Yes, we found pictures of women in bathrooms and some of Abigail Hicks, Marjorie Best, and the woman murdered in Lake Placid in his apartment."

"Do you have him in custody?" Maddy asked.

"No, he took off and somehow has evaded our roadblocks."

Maddy looked over at Hannah, and she appeared tired. "You look like your mind is drifting. Do you want me to drive the rest?"

"No, I'll be okay," Hannah said. Maddy asked what led her to pursue a career in law enforcement.

"I lost my brother when I was sixteen to a bullet gone astray by a gangbanger. He was walking home from the store, and, just like that, he was gone. He always looked out for me. I became bitter and mean until my grandpa sat me down for a talk one day."

"He said, 'Hannah, when Marcus died, he left a hole in your heart, and all the good he gave you is spilling out. Don't let that happen, dear. Our family needs all that goodness to keep living through you. If you return it, you'll make the world a better place.'"

"I can still hear how he said it, softly and reverently. Grandpa was like a preacher as he got older. Anyway, law enforcement is my way of giving back."

She glanced over at Maddy. "How about you? Why did you become a cop?"

"A graveside promise," Maddy said. Hannah gave her a curious look. "My father was a detective with the Chicago PD, and someone murdered him. The day they buried him, I kneeled by his casket and promised I'd become a detective, just like him. And so, that's what I did."

They entered the village of Berry Lake, and it was late. The only lights were the streetlamps; the place looked abandoned. They approached the command center, and Maddy wondered if she'd made a mistake by telling Hannah of Whitfield.

She upholds the law as a senior agent with the FBI. She could accuse me of withholding evidence essential to an investigation. I used to abide by the law, too. But I always knew when to close my eyes. I wonder what she'll do.

Hannah pulled into the parking lot next to Maddy's Jeep. She turned off the engine and sat silently. Finally, she spoke.

"Please take care of yourself, friend," she said. She turned to Maddy and stuck out her hand with her palm facing her. Maddy reached out, interlocked her fingers with hers, and said, "You too, friend."

They got out, and Maddy went to her Jeep, but it didn't start. Hannah walked over to the driver's side as Maddy rolled open the window.

"Looks like you need a ride home."

"Yeah, looks like it." They hopped in Hannah's car, and when they reached Maddy's house, Hannah said, "If you give me your car keys, I'll have someone look at it tomorrow." Hannah left, and Maddy went inside and opened the pantry. She grabbed a bottle of Cabernet and poured a glass. Shutting off the lights, she sat in the dark, sipping the wine and replaying the day's events.

Thoughts of young Sherry Zerwillager rushed into her mind, and Maddy wondered how her family was feeling then. *Whitfield is leaving a swath of pain in his wake.* The bright spot of her day was coming to an understanding with Hannah, and she felt grateful she no longer had to deceive her. *Who knows,* she thought, *maybe we can become friends.*

Worn out after an emotionally trying day, she set the glass on the table and rested her head on the sofa. A noise outside startled her. She looked, and the figure of a man in a black ski mask stood outside the door, looking at her. Rolling onto the floor and crawling to the kitchen, she grabbed the Glock from the counter. A loud bang rang out as she stood. The window glass shattered, and her left upper arm exploded with pain. She fired, and her round ripped into the metal doorjamb. Before her head slammed on the ceramic floor, she heard the guy shout and saw him reach over his right shoulder as though a piece of shrapnel had struck him.

Laying with her head aching and her arm burning up, she thought the guy had taken off, unaware of her vulnerable condition. She tried inching her way to the phone, but the room spun. With each move of her head, she'd lose touch with her surroundings, and finally, she lay still. Her mind was fuzzy, and in her half-conscious state, she could only see silhouettes in the darkness.

The beeping of three numbers on the handset of a telephone brought her to consciousness, and she heard, "Nine-one-one, what's your emergency?" Opening her eyes, she saw the image of a young girl before her in the darkness, holding the phone to her ear. It was Phoebe.

"This is Maddy Reynolds. I'm at my home and need medical attention. Send help. Contact Hannah Bates at the FBI and tell her Whitfield was here." The woman asked questions, but Maddy couldn't respond. Phoebe took the phone, pushed the button, and ended the call. The girl held Maddy's hand as she lay in pain.

Phoebe didn't speak as time passed. The sound of tires crunching gravel in the driveway snapped the girl's head. Turning to Maddy and leaning over, she gently kissed her forehead before slipping into darkness.

Lightheaded and confused, the pain in Maddy's head was more significant than the burning in her arm. She was semiconscious as she waited for someone to appear and felt overshadowed by a powerful sense of her life's purpose. The guardians of time were fading, merging the past and present. She was twelve, thirty, forty-four, and although death had worn many faces during her lifetime, she saw how he was always present.

Voices in the darkness tried to break through, and she heard, "Maddy, can you hear me? It's Hannah. Can you tell me what happened?"

Barely able to speak, Maddy muttered, "Whitfield is in the woods; move quickly."

CHAPTER FIFTEEN

Hannah

Hannah watched as the medical techs lifted Maddy into the back of the ambulance. The night felt eerily ominous as she inhaled the cool air and saw a gibbous moon hanging overhead.

"We found this hanging on the doorknob," Allen said, handing her a locket. Hannah took it, and an inscription said, *Happy Graduation, Sherry. Love, Mom and Dad.* Inside was a picture of a smiling girl of five in a blue dress with no front teeth. Another inscription read: *Sherry's first day of school.* She shook her head, and her eyes watered; Hannah knew what it was. *It's Sherry Zerwillager's high school graduation gift from her parents.* She wondered how many other mementos Whitfield had left for Maddy.

"We have people in the woods and roadblocks on Route Three," Allen said. "I'm heading down with one of the search crews now." He started for the woods as Hannah dialed her boss.

"Ben, it's Hannah. Whitfield went to Reynolds' home tonight. They exchanged gunfire, and she was wounded in her left upper arm. The wound doesn't appear serious, but she fell and hit her head. The medical people think she has a concussion and may have cracked her skull."

"Do you have a bead on Whitfield?" he asked.

"We have people in the woods and roadblocks set up on Route Three. Maddy's vehicle was not at the house, so he likely assumed the place was empty.

"Then why was he there?"

"He left her a piece of jewelry that belonged to Sherry Zerwillager. I think he's been leaving her keepsakes from his victims."

"Shit, Hannah, that's why he's in Berry Lake. He wants Reynolds."

"I think so," she said.

"You better post an agent to stand guard over her at whatever hospital she'll be at," he said.

"Will do." Hannah hung up, took a deep breath, sighed, and looked toward the woods where her team pursued Amos Whitfield. It was dark, and she was alone on Maddy's deck when flashes of light lit up the woods, and loud pops followed. Voices shouted. She couldn't tell what they were saying, but thought she heard someone yell, "He's hit!"

She dialed Allen's number to check what was happening; he didn't answer. Putting her hand to her head, she pushed her hair back as her chest tightened into a knot. Finally, her phone rang, and a man whose voice she didn't recognize huffed out words.

"This is Owens. Allen Bowers is down."

Hannah's heart dropped into her stomach. "How bad is he?"

"We don't know; we're bringing him out now."

She called for another ambulance and went to the end of the field to meet them. Flashlights shined, and the silhouettes of four men carrying a body became visible. They stepped out of the woods, and Hannah gasped when she saw Allen's head dangling.

"Bring him up to the house!" she shouted, following them across the field. "Place him on the deck and locate blankets inside," she directed. Someone flashed a light on Allen's face, and blood dripped from a hole beneath his right eye. An agent checked for a pulse and looked at Hannah.

"He's gone."

Kneeling, covering her mouth, she whispered, "Oh, Allen." Agent Owens talked over her shoulder as she looked in disbelief at the young man she'd mentored and cared for.

"Whitfield was waiting for us," Owens said. "It seemed as if he wanted to target one of us. He shot once, and Allen went down, then the guy disappeared. We fired several rounds in pursuit but lost him. He must have familiarized himself with the area ahead of time."

Numb and gazing at Allen's swollen face, Hannah wasn't listening. The words Allen had recently spoken repeated in her head. *I'm unsure how I'll do when it all comes down for me, and we both know it will.*

An ambulance arrived, and two med techs at once checked for signs of life. One glanced at the other and shook his head.

"Let us take him," a tech said to Hannah. She stood, moved aside, and watched them put Allen on a gurney. "We're bringing him to the medical examiner's office," the guy said.

Brian Owens was the next senior agent. He stood near to her, seemingly afraid to speak. Finally, he said, "Should we continue pursuing him?"

Hannah was struggling to shake off what had just happened. "I'm sorry. What did you say?" she asked.

"Should we send our people further into the woods after Whitfield?"

"No," she said. "Pull everyone out. In the dark like this, Whitfield will pick us off one at a time with our flashlights and his shooting skills. Give the order, but don't go anywhere." Owens stepped away for a moment and gave the order using his cell.

"Brian," she said. "Take two agents and head to Ernie Bajorek's home. If he's there, bring him to the command center. If he's not, call me immediately. He may be the guy we've been chasing, so be careful."

Brian got in a vehicle and departed. Hannah watched as people emerged from the trees and instructed them to gather.

"We've lost one of our own tonight," she said. "We'll remember this night for the rest of our lives. I want everyone back at the command center. You are to call someone you love. That's an order."

The young FBI agents quietly headed to the cars, leaving Hannah. When she was finally alone, she gazed at a gibbous moon reflecting on the waters of Berry Lake as a breeze blew into her face. *It's so perfect,* she thought. *But Allen Bowers is no more. His wife will be a widow, and his unborn child will grow up without a father.*

•   •   •

As she drove back to the command center, her cell phone rang, and it was Brian Owens.

"We're at the Bajorek home, and Ernie isn't here. His wife Chelsea is inside with an agent and said he's in New York City on business."

"Please find out his current location in the city and check if he is available by phone now," Hannah said.

"She says she doesn't know which hotel he's staying at. He goes there a lot on business and makes his arrangements. He doesn't always answer his cell and is due here on Friday."

"Get the details about his profession," Hannah said. "Find out the names of his associates and request a copy of his income tax return. If she refuses, inform her we'll get a search warrant."

"Will do," Owens said.

Hannah hung up, dreading the calls she had to make to her boss and Hellen Bowers, Allen's wife.

CHAPTER SIXTEEN

Maddy

The rain pattered on the hospital room window; it was a dark July morning, and Maddy lay staring out with her arm bandaged and head throbbing. She wondered what she'd tell Adam and, worse still, her daughter. She worried most for the child in the woods. She couldn't forget the sensation of Phoebe's warm hands comforting her as she kneeled next to her. A knock and a woman dressed in a pantsuit entered.

"Hi, Ms. Reynolds; I'm Rosemary Rodriguez from the FBI, and I will guard your room during the day while you're in the hospital."

Maddy said hello and tried to smile, but even that hurt. The woman nodded, walked out, and Maddy returned her gaze to the outside again, thinking of Phoebe.

She must have been nearby and heard the gunshots. I can't believe she showed up when she did. The dankness outside was as dark as the gloom she felt. Her eyes grew heavy, and she was nearly asleep when a man in blue scrubs entered the room. He was wearing sneakers, and a stethoscope hung from his neck.

"I'm Doctor Zingaro. How's the head?"

"It feels like something has shaken loose inside and rattles around every time I move or talk."

"That's fairly normal for someone who's just had a concussion. You had quite a fall."

"I was completely off balance, trying to fire a weapon as I fell and couldn't free my arms to break the fall. What about the wound on my arm?" she asked.

"The bullet took some flesh, but the scar will make you look tough." He chuckled. Maddy thought of her scars from past altercations and that she was tough enough.

"How long before the headaches go away?"

"It depends. A few days or months. Concussions are funny like that."

Shit! Maddy wondered how she'd go up against Whitfield feeling the way she did. "Be patient," he said. "Hope for the best. I want to observe your head pain for a few days." He looked at her chart. "In the meantime, we'll give you something to make you comfortable. Try to enjoy your stay," he said before walking out.

This is just fucking great. The phone rang. Reaching over and grabbing it, she said hello.

"Maddy, it's Adam." *Oh shit.*

"Are you okay?" he asked.

"Yes, I have a flesh wound on my left arm and a headache. Other than that, I'm fine. How did you find out?"

"I've been in law enforcement for over twenty years. I have many spies."

Maddy laughed and said she wished one of those spies had been at her house the night before and warned her Whitfield was coming.

"I can't believe this is happening," Adam said, frustrated. "What are you going to do?"

"I don't know yet. I need to see if these headaches go away. Then I'll resume my workout routine."

"Why did I have to fall in love with someone like you?" he said. "It's strange, but the very thing I love about you is the exact thing I hate about you right now—your courage!" Maddy laughed.

"That's funny. The quality about you I fell in love with keeps me in love with you now—your ability to accept me for who I am."

"We're quite a couple, aren't we?" he said. "All tattered and broken."

"Yeah, but even broken, we're a formidable force," she laughed.

"I love you, Maddy," Adam said.

"I love you too," she said before they hung up. She returned the phone to the table and sighed, wondering what might happen next. *Is Whitfield audacious enough to approach me in the hospital? I wish I had my weapon.* She suspected the FBI had taken the Glock she used to fire at Whitfield, but she had another. She reached for the phone again, put it on her lap, and dialed Rose.

"It's Maddy," she said when Rose answered.

"Oh, Maddy, I heard what happened."

"I'm in the Saranac Lake hospital and need a big favor."

"Sure, anything," Rose said.

"I need my weapon. I feel very unsafe without it."

"Okay, I just talked to Julie and Reverend Dietrich about visiting, and I'll bring it when we come."

"You can't tell anyone, not even them," Maddy said. "You'll have to hide it somehow. Here's what you need to do." Maddy explained where to find the metal box in her bedroom closet and gave her the combination to the lock. "Thanks, Rose, I owe you for this," she said.

"Anything for a friend," Rose said.

Maddy rolled onto her side, trying to find a comfortable position, and finally did. She fell asleep to the sound of rain and dreamed of shadowy faces. They were the faces that haunted her sleep during times of trouble since her father's murder. In her dream, for the first time, she realized the shadows were not evil but beings motivating her to act.

She didn't run from them as usual, nor did she hide. While dreaming, she welcomed them for the first time in her life. They were the parts of herself Zep had talked of—representing the killer in her. She had despised those parts. It felt strange to accept they were good and protected her.

The window shook, and her eyes opened as a long, rumbling thunder ended its drum roll. She lay still, contemplating what she'd learned in the dream. *Every event in my life has led me to this point.*

I never saw my purpose. I continuously moved from one crisis to another, barely making it out alive. Cupid caused me to move to Berry Lake, and that saved those young girls from sex trafficking at The Glades. It's strange how that worked out. She was tying together the missing pieces in her own life.

A knock at the door, and Hannah Bates entered.

"Hey," Hannah said, walking over with a lifeless expression and sitting in a chair. Maddy had never seen her so distraught.

"Why is it I feel something awful has happened," Maddy said.

Hannah shook her head and said, "Just after you left in the ambulance last night, Whitfield killed Allen Bowers."

"Oh, Hannah, I'm sorry."

"Yeah, he stayed hidden in the trees, and when Allen came up near, he shot him in the face." She fought her tears and said, "His wife is five months pregnant."

"I'm so sorry," Maddy said again. "He was a pleasant young man, and I know you liked him."

After a brief silence, Hannah asked, "How are you feeling?"

"I'm okay. The doctors want to observe me, but I'll be fine."

Hannah reached over and handed her the necklace with a locket.

"It belonged to Sherry Zerwillager. We found it on your doorknob, and it's the reason Whitfield came to your house last night. He probably saw that your car wasn't there and thought you weren't home." Maddy gazed at it in her hand, thinking, *That motherfucker needs to die!* Hannah wondered if Whitfield had left any more souvenirs for her.

"Beverly Arnold's leather necklace is in my dresser drawer, and Abigail Hicks's kidney is in the freezer in my basement."

"Geez, Maddy, he's coming after you hard. He wants you dead."

"I know," she said, handing the locket back. "Someone has to stop him, Hannah. I'm afraid Phoebe will be next."

"If he hasn't killed her already," Hannah said.

"She's been coming around my place. I've been leaving food out for her, and sometimes, when I return, it's gone. She's stayed clear of me until last night. When I was half out of it, lying on the kitchen floor, she appeared, dialed nine-one-one for me, and held my hand until you arrived. She's alive, alright, but now that I'm not there, I don't know where she'll go."

Is Ernie Bajorek still a person of interest?" Maddy asked.

"Very much so. We went to his home last night after we left your place, and his wife said he was in New York City on business. We've checked into his business dealings, and he's shady—runs a lot of high-stakes scams and moves around a lot."

"How about the tailor, Stanley Hartman?" Maddy asked. "Any more on him?"

"You're not considering going rogue, are you?" Hannah asked.

"I just want to know who's trying to kill me," Maddy said.

Hannah gave her a suspicious grin before saying she needed to get back. "We can protect you while you're in the hospital, but unless you let us put units at your home and a guard with you wherever you go, you'll be on your own when you leave here."

Maddy put out her hand. "Goodbye, friend," she said when Hannah took it.

"Being friends with someone with headstrong ways like you will not be easy," Hannah said, smiling. "Goodbye, Maddy."

The rain stopped, and the sun's rays broke through as Maddy pondered what to tell her daughter. She decided she couldn't put it off any longer, picked up the phone, and called Amber.

"Hi, honey," she said when Amber answered.

"Hi, Mom. I'm sorry for getting mad at you when we last talked," she said. "I guess I go overboard sometimes worrying about you."

"You have a right to feel that way. I feel like I've been a never-ending source of worry for you."

"Oh, Mom, it's like you said, you couldn't control what has happened to you, although I wish you'd turn and run sometimes instead of always barreling head-on into a fight."

"Amber, there's something you should know," Maddy said.

"What is it?"

"I'm calling you from a hospital. Before you get too concerned, I'm alright. I slipped and fell in my kitchen and hit my head. It's just a slight concussion."

"Oh, my God, Mom, how did you do that? Had you been drinking?"

"No, I wasn't drinking. I—ahh, I—ahh."

"You what?" Amber shouted impatiently.

"I was firing my weapon at a guy shooting at me from outside, and I slipped."

"What? Are you shitting me? I have to go, Mom," she said. "I'll call you soon."

Fuck, that didn't go well. She started self-flagellation as a mother when the phone rang again, and picking it up, she heard the muffled voice. "Your days are numbered, Reynolds." He hung up, and Maddy's heart pounded. She knew Rosemary Rodriguez, sitting in the hall guarding the door, was no match for Whitfield, so she called Rose, feeling helpless and vulnerable.

"Hello," Rose answered.

"Do you have any idea when you'll be coming to visit me?"

"Reverend Dietrich is on his way to pick me up now. He'll be here any minute," Rose said.

Maddy asked if she'd gotten her Glock. "Yes. It's at the bottom of a basket of baked goods I made for you. No one will know."

"Great, thank you for doing this." Maddy sat up, rolled her legs over the side, and stood, holding onto the bed. Her eyes squinted from the pain in her head. She took a step, then another. *I have to push my way through this,* she said to herself. Her head pounded as she reached the far wall, held it briefly, then turned around and gingerly returned to the bed. "That's once," she said. She repeated ten times before flopping onto the mattress. *This could take forever,* she thought.

She rested, got up again, went to the closet, brought the box with her street clothes to the bed, and dressed. *I will see myself as others see me,* she thought. *I don't want anyone to see me as a helpless patient with my ass hanging out of a hospital gown.* Once dressed, she sat in one of the three chairs and, with her head throbbing, waited.

Shortly after, she heard familiar voices. Rose, Julie, and Reverend Dietrich stepped into the room. Rose's face lit up when she saw Maddy, and she rushed over, gently hugging her. "I brought you something to snack on while you're here," she said, turning and placing a basket on a table.

"Have a seat," Maddy said. "I'm afraid one of you will have to sit on the bed." The Reverend said he'd stand.

"How are you feeling?" Rose asked.

"Just a slight headache. The doctor wants to keep me here for a few days to ensure I'm okay." Maddy wanted to divert attention from herself and asked about the others.

"Things are creepy in town," Julie said. "I had to close the antique shop because no one seems to leave their homes since all this started."

"Yes, it's extraordinary," the Reverend said. "This Sunday, my sermon will focus on courage in the face of danger."

"All anyone can talk about at the diner is you," Rose said. "People believe that if it happened to you, it can happen to anyone."

With his arms crossed, the Reverend asked Rose if anyone had seen the little girl in the woods.

"People have glimpsed her; some say she's been stealing food from their homes. Your assistant, Amy Chapman, said she knows someone who's seen her three times."

"Oh, Amy. I need to speak with her about exaggerating," Dietrich said. The reverend looked at Maddy and asked her how Adam was doing.

"He's doing well, but he's worried about me."

"I bet you can't wait until he comes home," he said.

"Yes, I can't wait. Is the town fair still happening?" Julie said the town was going ahead with it.

"That reminds me," Dietrich said. "Are you ladies still planning to bring baked goods to the church booth?" Julie and Rose said they were. "Wonderful. The proceeds from our baked goods sale are a necessary source of income for the church fund." Rose said she was making apple pies, and Julie said she'd bring a pineapple cobbler.

"When did they say you'd be coming home?" Rose asked.

"It looks like it'll be Thursday."

A knock, and a nurse entered. "Oh, hello, everyone," she said. "Would you mind stepping outside while I take some vitals?"

"I need to head back," the Reverend said. "We should get going."

They said goodbye, and when Maddy hugged Rose, she whispered, "Thank you for the baked goods."

CHAPTER SEVENTEEN

Marjorie

Marjorie lay on the sofa, staring into space, unable to remember how long she'd been there, when the front door opened. It was her husband.

"Have you taken the pills Doctor Peters gave you?" he asked.

"No…I mean, yes…I mean, I don't know." The pills made her tired and forgetful.

"I stopped by Lena's and picked up a couple of meatloaf meals for dinner," he said. Marjorie hadn't cooked since the killer left the heart at her front door. She sat up, put her hands on her knees, and shook her head. "I can't keep taking those pills. I'm useless when I feel this way."

Lester went to the kitchen with the paper bag. Silverware and dishes rattled and clattered as he set the table. When Marjorie walked in and sat, he placed a glass of iced tea on the table for her and a beer for himself before sitting down.

"I need to return to normal," she said. "This morning, I felt woozy while picking raspberries and had to lie down. By the way, someone picked the bushes nearly bare."

"It's probably those damn raccoons again," Lester said.

"Well, tomorrow, no more pills. I can't keep living like a zombie. I will clean this house, cut some rhubarb from behind the barn, and bake a pie. Damn it, that's what I'll do." Her husband smiled and said he'd cut the rhubarb for her.

"I want to do it," she insisted. "I'll bring the shotgun."

Marjorie noticed Lester's mood as they started eating. He had several moods that were indistinguishable from others, but not this. This one meant something was wrong.

"What is it?" she asked. Lester put his fork and knife on the table and looked at her. "It's Maddy Reynolds; that guy shot her at her house. She's not dead, but she's in the hospital in Saranac Lake."

"Maddy?" she whispered disbelievingly, dropping her head into her hands. Maddy was the bravest person she knew; that man had taken her down. *If Maddy can't stand up to him, who can?* She lost her appetite and felt shaky when she stood. "I'm not hungry, Lester. I'm going upstairs." With each step, the weight of her body grew heavier. It was as if Maddy's defeat meant Marjorie's destruction was inevitable. Despite the early hour, she prepared for bed and hid under the covers.

The following day, she opened her eyes, and her head ached as if she had a hangover. She sat up, determined not to ingest any more anti-anxiety pills, but the room spun. Standing, she got her bearings, went to the bathroom, and flushed the little white monsters into the toilet. *That's the end of that!*

Marjorie went to the kitchen, filled a teapot, and turned on the burner. While waiting for the water to boil, she thought of Maddy. It was hard to comprehend Whitfield had gotten the best of her. She sighed and pushed the unpleasant notion away, focusing on her plans for the day. *A rhubarb pie! I'm going to make a rhubarb pie.* Making the pie was her way of escaping her fear of Amos Whitfield.

She went to the cupboard and pulled out one of her three pie dishes. She had four, but when she put a pie on the porch to cool, someone stole it. After finishing her tea, she went to a cabinet and took her gardening gloves and a knife to cut the rhubarb.

Grabbing the shotgun from the broom closet and carrying it to the yard with the bag and the knife, she started toward the side of the barn where the rhubarb grew thick. The barn door was open two feet, so she dropped the bag and knife, lifted the twelve gauge, and eased her way to the entrance. She stepped inside, moving the door open with the tip of the barrel. It was dark except for light streaming through a few cracks in the barn wood.

Marjorie put her index finger on the safety when she heard a sound in the horse stall. Snapping her head around, she pointed the gun in its direction, eased her way closer, and pushed the door open with the barrel. A redheaded girl with her back against the wall stood, her eyes wide and mouth open.

"Please don't shoot me."

"Oh, dear Lord, child, I will not hurt you," Marjorie said, kneeling and placing the gun on the ground.

The girl looked as if she was going to bolt, and as Marjorie raised her arms to embrace her, she ran past and out of the barn. Marjorie watched as she entered the woods behind the house, thinking it must be the girl from Maddy's.

Returning to the house to put the shotgun inside, she sat on the porch step, hoping the girl was watching from the woods. She remembered Lester said her name was Phoebe and thundered, "I'm going to wait here for you, Phoebe! I won't hurt you! I want to help you!" Her words echoed through the tree. The only other sounds were birds singing and an occasional car driving by. "I'm friends with Maddy Reynolds. Is she your friend, too?"

A movement turned Marjorie's head. In the distance, she saw the girl stepping through the trees toward the house. Phoebe cautiously approached the yard as a deer ready to flee from danger. Marjorie's heart pounded, afraid of making a wrong move and sending her back into the forest. The girl stopped fifteen feet away.

"Is Maddy here?" she asked.

"Not right now, but she's supposed to visit me soon."

"What's your name?" the girl asked.

"My name is Marjorie. Are you hungry? Come inside, and I'll make you something to eat."

Marjorie stood, went to the door, and held it open as Phoebe waited hesitantly. Finally, she walked up the stairs and into the house. Pulling back a chair at the kitchen table, Marjorie gestured for Phoebe to sit.

"Do you have Rice Krispies?" the girl asked.

"No, but do you like pancakes?" Phoebe nodded. "How about a glass of cold milk?"

"Yes, please." The child's gaze fixed on Marjorie as she made the pancakes. *She is so perfect,* Marjorie thought after she brought the food to the table and Phoebe started eating. She finished, downed the last of her milk, and belched.

"Excuse me," the girl said. "Do you have a television?" she asked.

"Yes, right here in the next room." Phoebe got comfortable on the carpet, and Marjorie flipped stations until she found *Hey Arnold!* Marveling at the girl's laughter as she focused entirely on the characters, Marjorie delighted in her every movement. Phoebe was utterly present in the moment.

The show ended, and going to the sofa to sit beside Marjorie, Phoebe gazed at her as though she wanted to ask her something. Seemingly unable to articulate what was on her mind, she laid her head on Marjorie's lap until she fell asleep. Marjorie sat mesmerized. The stillness and the child's presence made everything feel magical. *So, this is how it feels to be a mother.*

The clock on the mantle ticked away the hours until Marjorie realized Lester would be home soon, and he and Phoebe needed to know about one another. She gently ran her fingers through the girl's hair until she moved, and her eyes opened. Sitting up and stretching, she yawned.

"Can I take a bath?" Phoebe asked.

"Sure, you can. But I want you to know Lester will come home soon. He's my husband."

"I know what that is; he's your friend, right?"

"Yes," Marjorie laughed. "Let's go upstairs and start your bath water."

When the bath was ready, Phoebe undressed and stepped into the tub. "Do you have any bubbles?"

"Bubbles? Oh, bubbles! I think I do." Marjorie went to the closet and found bubble bath soap she'd gotten as a gift but had never used.

She poured the powder into the water, and Phoebe moved it around until pink bubbles covered her. "When you're ready, call me, and I'll wash your hair."

After putting Phoebe's clothes in the washing machine, she dug out things to wear and called Lester at the hardware store.

"You'll find a surprise when you get home," she said. "Please keep calm, and I'll explain everything after dinner." She spoke cautiously, wanting to hide the girl from the FBI, who tapped her phone.

Phoebe called out that she was ready. After washing her hair, Marjorie set her up in makeshift pajamas, and the girl returned to her position on the floor in front of the television.

"Do you like spaghetti and meatballs?" Marjorie said. Phoebe looked up as if unaware of the words' meaning. "Will you try it if I make it?" Phoebe nodded.

Marjorie went to the kitchen and began heating her frozen homemade sauce. The living room door opened, she ran out, and Lester looked confused. Phoebe glanced at him, said "Hi," and returned to her show.

"This is the surprise," Marjorie said. She asked him to join her in the kitchen, and he glanced at the girl on the living room floor as he walked past her.

"Before you say anything, hear me out," she insisted. She put her hands on the table. "Her name is Phoebe, and she's the girl who was at Maddy Reynolds's house. She's been staying in our barn. I went out to cut the rhubarb, and she ran into the woods, but I coaxed her into the house, and she's been with me all afternoon. She was initially afraid but calmed down and feels comfortable here."

Lester looked as if he was trying to compute overwhelming amounts of information when Phoebe erupted in laughter in the next room. He turned his head, bewildered.

"She's been in the woods all these days," Marjorie said. "She was starving and exhausted. She needs care, and I can give it to her, Lester. We both can give it to her."

"The FBI is actively searching the area for this girl."

"I know, but if they take her, they'll put her in a foster home. She feels safe here. Just for a few days, Lester." He sighed and gave his wife a look that told her he knew how much she needed the child.

"Just until tomorrow," he said.

"Okay, we'll discuss it tomorrow, but for tonight, let's enjoy her." Smiling, she got up and put the spaghetti in the boiling water. Lester went to the living room to read his newspaper. Phoebe laughed hysterically at her program. When Marjorie entered to announce that the food was on the table, Lester sat with the newspaper on his lap, gazing at the girl, smiling.

"It's time to eat," she said. Phoebe jumped to her feet and said she was starving. She bolted to the kitchen. Lester and Marjorie exchanged glances as the wiry redhead ran past them.

"This is spaghetti?" Phoebe asked. "How do you eat it?"

"Watch me," Lester said. He showed her how to twirl the pasta strands. Phoebe tried, but the spaghetti slipped from the fork.

"I'll starve if I have to eat it like that."

"Just eat it any way that works," Marjorie said. "I have other pajamas if you make a mess." Phoebe began slurping the noodles into her mouth.

"Wow, this is good. What are those round things?"

"Those are meatballs," Lester said, placing one in her dish. "Try it."

She ate the meatball, finished the spaghetti on her plate, and sat back. "I'm full." Red sauce dotted her face and pajama top. After inhaling deeply, she looked at Lester and asked, "Do you have any cards?"

"Cards?"

"You know, cards so we can play rummy?" Lester acted unsure of the girl.

"Where are the cards, Marj?" he asked.

"They're in the end table drawer in the living room."

"Do you want to play?" Phoebe asked him with excited anticipation.

"Okay," he said. Marjorie cleaned Phoebe's face before they went to the living room. While clearing the table, she reflected on the energy that had sparked a new sense of excitement in her home. She thought of Lester's one-night policy. *I said we'd discuss it, but I didn't say I agreed,* she told herself. She finished in the kitchen and read a magazine while Lester and Phoebe played rummy.

"I won," Phoebe shouted, startling her. She lay the magazine on her lap as Lester looked over, smiling. She couldn't remember the last time her husband was as lighthearted.

It got late, and Marjorie said they should start getting ready for bed. Focusing on the cards, Phoebe raised her hand and said she was nearly out. Soon, the game ended, and Phoebe leaned back, yawning. "That was fun, Lester," she said. Marjorie brought her to the spare bedroom and helped her out of the sauce-stained clothes and into clean pajamas.

"I'm afraid to sleep alone," Phoebe said. "Will you sleep with me?"

"Sure," Marjorie said. "Do you want to tell me what you're afraid of?"

Phoebe crossed her arms. "No one was there when I went to my grandma's house. Do you know Abigail Hicks?"

"Yes, I know your grandma," Marjorie said.

"Do you know what happened to her?"

Moving closer, Marjorie took her hands and looked into her eyes.

"She died, Phoebe."

"How did she die?"

"A man killed her," she said. Phoebe looked to the side, lay her head on Marjorie's lap, and wept. Marjorie ran her hand over her hair, trying to comfort her, but Phoebe didn't stop whaling until she fell asleep. As Marjorie lay beside her that evening, Phoebe occasionally awakened and whimpered herself into slumber.

CHAPTER EIGHTEEN

Hannah

Hannah was on the phone with her boss, asking for more agents to cover the upcoming town fair.

"Can't you get them to cancel that damn event?" Harris said.

"We've tried, but it's all paid for, and they won't do it," she said.

"Did you tell them that Whitfield uses situations like that to steal away victims?"

"We have, Ben, but they said it's our job to keep people safe."

"Okay, I'll send you the extra agents. By the way, who are you putting in Allen Bowers' spot?"

"Brian Owens," she said. "I think he's ready." Hannah ran her hand over her hair and hung up, noticing Sara standing nearby, waiting. "What is it?"

"A man reported an abandoned Subaru near Wheeler's Cliff."

"Did he give any more details?"

"He said someone covered it with branches."

"Where's Brian Owens?" Hannah asked.

"He just returned from interviewing Sherry Zerwillager's parents and is in the lunchroom."

Brian walked out, eating a sandwich. "Finish it in the car," Hannah said. "We're on our way to an abandoned Subaru, and you can debrief me about your visit on the way."

Brian took bites from his turkey sandwich as Hannah drove. "Discussing a deceased child's life with her parents might be one of the hardest things I'll have to do in this job," he said as he opened a folder on his lap. "Raising a daughter to eighteen, only to lose her to a serial killer, is horrifying. But they were cooperative, and I learned a lot." He picked up a sheet of paper and started reading.

"Sherry was an honor student and aspired to teach music. She also was athletic, competed in the New York State Games in track during her senior year, and was active in the church choir. She was cantor during the masses at St. Matthew's Church, and her parents said she had the voice of an angel."

Brian placed the paper on his lap, wrapped the turkey sandwich's remains in a napkin, crumpled it, and set it aside.

"Sherry attended a marathon runners' summer camp in May. In June, she participated with other church members in a concert choir competition in Saratoga. She was to attend a voice seminar at Syracuse University in August, but of course, didn't make it."

"Good job, Brian," Hannah said. "Tomorrow, get a list of attendees at the track and field event and the Saratoga choir competition. Let's try to connect a few dots."

They drove a rutted road a hundred yards into tall pines and arrived where a local man, Henry Larkin, stood holding a leash as his beagle thrashed around. Two carloads of FBI agents exited and walked to them.

"We were heading home from a walk in the woods," Larkin said. "Suddenly, Jeter started acting crazy. He dragged me to that thicket, and when we got close, the smell of something rank nearly made me vomit. I pulled away some branches and saw the car, so I called the sheriff."

Several agents climbed down a twenty-yard hill toward the thicket; Hannah followed. They pulled off the remaining tree branches and carefully opened each car door with gloved hands. The stench was powerful. Brian opened the back hatch, and a partly decomposed man's body with a large gash in his throat lay on his side.

"Let's get forensics over here," Hannah said as she covered her mouth. "This has to be Stanley Hartman." She climbed back to the road, and she and Brian started for the command center while the others stayed.

"Where are we now?" Brian asked as he drove.

Hannah summarized her thoughts. "The guy in the car is Whitfield's decoy and is likely Stanley Hartman. Hartman was a voyeur who got his jollies by taking photos of ladies in bathrooms. Whitfield cleverly set him up by adding photos of his victims to Hartman's bathroom pictures. He knew we'd be checking the guy out and would find his collection. The bastard is one cunning son-of-a-bitch."

"So, what's our next step?" Brian asked.

"We start over, reassess all recent male arrivals, and put a full-court press on investigating Ernie Bajorek's location. I want everyone on it and no stone to go unturned."

They entered the school cafeteria. Brian started assigning teams to the remaining eight people for reassessment. He and Sara worked on taking a deeper dive into the information gathered on Bajorek.

CHAPTER NINETEEN

Maddy

Sheriff Collins waited in his cruiser outside the hospital as an orderly rolled Maddy to the car. He exited the vehicle and held the door open for her.

"That's a silly tradition," she said when she got in, and he drove off. He looked at her quizzically. "You know," she said, "why bother with a wheelchair when you can walk?" Collins laughed.

"Sheriff, I don't know your first name," Maddy said.

"Lenard. My name is Lenard."

"Lenard, it's nice that we finally get to meet. Thanks for the ride."

"Please call me Lenny; only my mother calls me Lenard."

Maddy smiled and said, "I know how you feel. My mother was the only person who ever called me Madison. Do you have a family, Lenny?"

"Sure do. A wife and three boys under ten. We got our hands full."

"I bet you do," Maddy said, laughing.

Out of the blue, Lenny said, "I wonder who will be next?" Maddy looked at him, and he said worriedly, "Maynard Krantz and I were friends. He was rough in the eyes of some, but he coached my son's baseball team and was gentle and kind with kids. Having your throat cut is an awful way to die. You can't even scream for help because of the blood in your windpipe."

"I got the impression he was rather fond of Marjorie Best," Maddy said.

"He was at my place one night, had a few too many, and said they were an item in high school. He told me she was the only woman he'd ever loved."

"Yet they didn't end up together," she said.

"No, Maynard said her father hated him, and he never understood why. He said he lived daily in the shadow of his love for Marjorie." Lenny sadly looked at Maddy. "It reminds me of something Tennyson wrote in one of his poems. 'Dear as remember'd kisses after death, And sweet as those by hopeless fancy feign'd. On lips that are for others; deep as love, Deep as first love, and wild with all regret; O Death in Life, the days that are no more!'"

"Gee, Lenny, I wouldn't have taken you for a poetry lover," Maddy said.

"Yeah, I'm a real anomaly. I was a community college literature major before becoming a cop."

She gazed at him, realizing people were more than what meets the eye. She asked if they were still pursuing two persons of interest.

"We eliminated one yesterday," he said. "Stanley Hartman showed up with his throat cut. It wasn't a pretty sight."

"I see," she said. "Hartman must have been Whitfield's decoy. I guess that leaves Ernie Bajorek."

"Yeah, the FBI is hot and heavy after him."

Collins pulled his patrol car up to Maddy's house. "I'd like to take a walk-through," he said.

"Sure, no problem."

"Oh, Hannah asked me to give this to you." He reached into the back seat, grabbed a box, and handed it to Maddy. She lay it on her lap, opened it, and pulled out her Glock.

"Thanks," she said. She carried a bag given to her at the hospital and her weapon up the deck steps when she got out of the car. Collins walked behind her, and they stopped at the sliding glass door. Someone had replaced the shattered glass. She looked at Collins.

"Lester Best sent Stick Larson out here to take care of this for you," he said.

Emotions gathered in Maddy's throat. She resisted showing tears before the sheriff, yet she sincerely appreciated the kind gesture. Opening the door, she walked in, and someone had cleaned the blood from the kitchen floor. A note and daisies from her garden were on the table.

Lenny said he would look around the house. With his hand on his revolver, he stepped through her place. Maddy sat and pulled the note from under the glass with the flowers.

Maddy. Lester says there's no charge for fixing the door. Welcome home. Stick Larson. Thinking of how the people of Berry Lake had embraced her as one of their own, tears welled in Maddy's eyes.

"I'll check out the basement," Lenny said when he finished with the upstairs. She nodded, lost in her thoughts. *I need to stop at the hardware store and thank them.*

A loud bang that echoed throughout the house jolted Maddy. She grabbed her weapon and edged her way to the cellar door, holding the gun in firing position. Lunging around the doorway, ready to shoot, she saw two legs lying on the basement floor. Sunlight shined in from the open outside door.

Holding the Glock, she crept the stairs to the basement. The sheriff lay on his face. Blood streamed from the back of his head, and she ran to the door. A man wearing a black ski mask disappeared into the woods at the end of the field. Turning to Collins, she kneeled and tried to find a pulse but couldn't.

"Oh, dear God, Lenny," she said to him as she wept. "You took a bullet meant for me. You wondered who would be next and didn't know it would be you."

Stepping back, examining the position of the body, Maddy surmised the killer had been hiding behind the furnace. She studied the deadbolt lock on the door, and it was intact. She realized Whitfield had entered through the kitchen door before they repaired it. Her stomach knotted, her head ached, and nothing felt real. Pushing herself up the stairs, thinking of Lenny's three boys, she went to the kitchen and called Hannah Bates.

CHAPTER TWENTY

Hannah

"The son-of-a-bitch killed the sheriff," Hannah told her boss on the phone as she and Brian Owens sped to the Reynolds home. "The details are sketchy; I'll fill you in when we get there," she said before ending the call.

As Brian drove, Hannah felt charged with tension. *It's as if I'm reliving a nightmare. Only four days ago, Whitfield killed Allen behind the Reynolds home, and now it's Sheriff Collins.*

Looking at the young FBI agent driving the car wound tighter than the inside of a baseball, Hannah knew her anxious state wasn't helping matters. Trying to calm herself, she took deep breaths and told herself things weren't as dire as they appeared. *That's bullshit,* she finally acknowledged. *Things are spinning out of control.*

Three sheriff's cars waited with engines running and open doors when Brian pulled up outside Reynolds' house. The scene screamed of a tragedy. Hannah and Brian walked inside, and young Deputy Mott pointed at the basement stairs as he stood weeping. Hannah descended into the basement, and another deputy stood looking over Collins while Maddy sat on the floor near the body. Her elbows rested on her knees, her head on her clasped hands, and a Glock lay on the floor before her.

"Maddy!" she said.

Maddy looked up, shaking her head, and Hannah sat beside her.

"How did it happen?"

"He gave me a ride home from the hospital and offered to check out the house, but Whitfield hid behind the furnace."

"He's obsessed with killing you, Maddy. You're vulnerable in this house and need to stay elsewhere."

"I'm not leaving my home," Maddy said emphatically.

A deputy approached Hannah. "I called an ambulance and the medical examiner."

"Did he have a family?" she asked as she stood.

"A wife and three young kids," the deputy responded.

"We need someone to tell them."

"I should be the one," he said. "I'll wait until the medical examiner pronounces him dead, then go."

The sound of footsteps on the stairs turned their heads, and it was Tom Hartley, the medical examiner. He went to the body and kneeled. "Oh, Lenny," he said in a painful moan. Feeling for a pulse and checking Lenny's eyes, Hartley looked at Hannah with tears in his eyes.

"He's gone."

"We should go upstairs and have Tom deal with the body," Hannah suggested to Maddy. Hannah joined a group of agents in the kitchen, and Maddy went to the deck.

"We will not be pursuing the killer into the woods," Hannah told her agents. She wasn't about to lose any more of her team in a Whitfield turkey shoot. "Brian, have two helicopters scan the woods and set up roadblocks on Route Three."

Hannah looked outside when she finished with her people, and Maddy sat at the patio table with her arms crossed.

Hours had passed before the medical examiner took Lenny Collins's body away, and the agents finished their investigation. Hannah went outside, and Maddy sat in the same position, her arms still crossed; she hadn't moved.

"What will you do, Maddy?" she asked.

Maddy turned her head, glaring, and said, "This is my fight, Hannah. He knows I'm here, and I'm not running."

Having given up trying to dissuade Maddy Reynolds from standing her ground, Hannah stretched out her hand, looked into Maddy's eyes, and said, "God, be with you."

"Thank you, friend," Maddy said, clutching Hannah's hand.

As Brian Owens drove to the command center, Hannah watched as the late afternoon sunlight rested on the surrounding Berry Lake mountains. She thought she might never forget the look on Maddy's face as they carried Lenny Collins's body to the medical examiner's van. Her look was not what she expected. Throughout the years, Hannah had seen both sides of Reynolds. Most people saw her mild-mannered side. Few had seen the relentless warrior who fought to the death when cornered.

That person killed Cupid, a serial killer, in hand-to-hand combat and Sedgwick Neri, The Glades' enforcer, without a weapon. With a handgun, no one Hannah knew was a match for Reynolds. Maddy was a High Master Shooter, and her abilities were unparalleled. But Maddy hadn't worked to keep those skills since she moved to Berry Lake. Hannah questioned if she could measure up to Whitfield's reputation with a handgun.

It was anyone's guess what the ex-detective might do. The fighter within Reynolds would go down fighting rather than back away from confrontation. Hannah remembered her boss once told her that Reynolds had killed more bad guys than any FBI agents on their team had arrested. Maddy wouldn't back down, even if the outcome were uncertain. She dispelled any doubts when she said it was her fight.

Hannah dreaded the call she had to make to her boss. "Ben, it's Hannah," she said when he answered. "Things are getting crazier in Berry Lake. Whitfield killed Sheriff Collins at Reynolds' home. He'd come for Maddy and was hiding in the basement. The sheriff was checking the house, and he shot him. Reynolds refuses to leave her place."

"Of course she does," he said. "That woman won't back down, no matter what. What about Whitfield?"

"We've set up roadblocks and are searching the woods with helicopters, but we're not sending our people in after him."

"Any updates on Ernie Bajorek?" he asked.

"We've uncovered a money laundering scheme he's involved with. If he's in Berry Lake, he's not staying at his home; we've covered the place in every way possible."

"He might have an alternate hiding spot," Ben suggested. "If he does, it will be remotely located."

When they hung up, Hannah had a sinking feeling she was grasping at straws, and her boss knew it. She walked into the command center, determined to rethink her situation. *We must have missed something.*

CHAPTER TWENTY-ONE

Maddy

Maddy watched the last of the FBI vehicles move out of sight on her road after the medical examiner had taken the Sheriff's body away. She thought of the two men Whitfield killed at her place. *I need to get out of here.* She went to her Jeep and started driving. She held the steering wheel but wasn't paying attention as events of that morning played over and over in her head, and rage ripped at her insides.

Descending into the darkness of trees on an unfamiliar mountain road, it curved, dipped, and grew darker the further she went. She finally reached the light at the bottom and got out. A frothy stream moved over rocks beneath a wooden bridge. The sun shone, and the late afternoon sky was blue. She had never been there before but recognized the place. She walked over rocks and branches to the water's edge and sat on a fallen tree. The sun's warmth rested on her face, and birdsong filled the cloudless sky.

Wrapping her hands around herself, trying to keep her aching from spilling out, she thought, *There's been too much death in my life. It has followed me to Berry Lake, and people are dying because of me.*

The thought weighed heavily on her. The faces of Whitfield's victims flashed before her. Each life was unfinished, dreams unrealized, and vacant spaces left behind in loved ones' lives. She lingered in the sacred place, lost in thoughts of them, reluctant to leave. Feeling their presence wanting to tell her something, the sounds of the gurgling water mired their message. They muttered in unison, as in a chant, a phrase she didn't understand. *Wiz 262425* seemed to hide in the guttural sounds of the stream. *Wiz 262425, Wiz 262425.*

"What is that?" she wondered. The babbling sounds of the water soothed her, even though she didn't understand the phrase's meaning. Although Maddy wasn't religious, she never doubted otherworldly spiritual experiences when they occurred. She had them with her father and a deceased friend, Mary Thompson. They always provided something she needed, and even though she didn't understand its meaning, Maddy committed *Wiz 262425* to memory.

The sun began falling behind a hill, and a breeze chilled her body as if telling her it was time to go. She stood and started for her Jeep, feeling lost and alone. Stopping, she turned and envied the endless rambling stream.

Finding her way back to Route 3, she turned left toward Albany Medical Center instead of right toward home. The road brought her into endless dips and rises, twists and turns along the lonely way. Maddy felt empty. The forests, lakes, and mountains wept with her. She fled the city years ago to escape violence but couldn't outrun its grasp.

With her hands limply resting on the steering wheel, Maddy had lost strength, and her fight drained. She'd known sadness and fear before, but never had she experienced utter defeat as she had with Amos Whitfield.

She arrived at the hospital thinking of how things had worsened since her last visit. She asked the front desk for Adam. When he exited the elevator with a walker, he smiled and came to her. Maddy twisted her head to the side and wept.

Adam held her until she finally caught her breath, and she whispered in his ear, "Whitfield killed Sheriff Collins at our house today." Pulling his head back, he closed his eyes and shook his head.

"Let's sit," he said. He grabbed the walker, and they moved to their usual isolated spot. They sat, and he asked how it happened. When she explained, Adam dropped his head in his hands. "I can't believe this," he said.

"I didn't ask for this, Adam. And I'm not going to Denver, San Diego, or Utica. I'll be running for the rest of my life if I do. I have to face him in Berry Lake. It's the only logical choice."

"Logical? There's nothing logical about any of this," he said. Maddy looked away.

"I'm sorry. Perhaps this is a moment of change in our relationship," she said. Adam folded his arms and said nothing. He sat silently, gazing at her as if wondering what to say. "You've allowed me to be myself, even if you had reservations. It was what I loved about you."

He leaned over and held her. "Please don't use the past tense when you say that. I love you and won't try to change what you want to do." She'd missed his embrace, and at that moment, she needed him more than ever. Pulling out a tissue, she wiped her face.

"I love you too," she said. He ran his hand along her face.

"You look pale. Are you hungry?"

"I haven't eaten all day; I guess I am."

"Let's grab a bite in the cafeteria," he said. He pulled over the walker and stood, and they walked to a line, where each piled food onto a tray.

The hot soup was comforting. "It's hard to believe how much has changed," Maddy said as she ate.

"I guess that happens whenever a serial killer moves into a community," Adam said. "It's like a tapeworm, sucking out life from the inside."

Maddy said she missed their mornings together, having coffee and watching the sunrise over the mountains. He smiled, reached out, and held her hand.

He asked, "What will you do?"

"I'm going to stay on top of my game, be ready for him, and hope Hannah and her team take him down before I have to."

"Sometimes words just don't cut it," Adam said, reaching over and pulling her close. Leaning her head on his shoulder, they sat silently for the rest of the time. Finally, Maddy said she should head back.

Her mind was on Amos Whitfield as she drove home. Halfway there, her cell phone rang, and it was Jodi.

"Can you talk?" Jodi asked.

"Yeah, I'm on the long road to Berry Lake from Albany. I just visited with Adam." Maddy put the phone on hands-free, sat back, and took a deep breath, feeling the comfort of her friend's voice.

"Have they caught that guy?" Jodi asked.

"I'm afraid not," Maddy said. "He killed the local sheriff at my house today. He's closing in and is damn determined to kill me."

"It's hard to know what to say, Maddy," Jodi said. "You've been in the crosshairs of maniacs so many times. I'm sorry your life has been so difficult."

"I don't understand why it's this way," Maddy said. "We don't get to choose certain aspects of our lives. I can cower in fear and complain about my plight or face it with dignity. Ultimately, no matter what comes to be, I can be proud I chose the latter."

There was silence until Jodi spoke. "Beverly's funeral was yesterday. I went, and it was sad. She was so well loved."

"The Maiden and the Lily puzzle on my dining room table reminds me of her," Maddy said. "It doesn't look like I'll be working on it soon, dear friend."

"I'll tell you what," Jodi said. "Once this craziness ends and Whitfield is in jail, I'll visit you with a couple of bottles of wine, and we'll work on the puzzle together."

"I can't tell you how much I look forward to that," Maddy said.

When she hung up, she was nearing her home. Climbing her road, she pulled up, and the house starkly stood against the darkness of the night. She thought of Lenny, the father of three boys, lying on her basement floor. *It should have been me.* She grabbed the handgun and got out.

She stopped and stood in the darkness, listening for any sounds that might be the killer. Moving cautiously toward the steps, a cool breeze to her back, Maddy held the weapon in firing position as though a snake might lurch at her at any moment. She reached the door, unlocked it, and stepped into the house.

She needed to check the outside basement door and waited until her eyes grew accustomed to the darkness. At the top of the basement stairs, she stopped. She carefully opened the door. Hearing nothing, she gingerly walked down and turned on the light. No one was there. Checking the lock on the door, it was intact. She pushed the safety on the weapon and returned upstairs.

She closed the blinds, made a fire, opened a bottle of wine, and sat on the sofa with the gun beside her. It was after midnight. She was too wired to sleep; it felt like an eternity had passed since she'd left the hospital with the sheriff that morning. Maddy pondered how to find Amos Whitfield with limited information.

She remembered Rose saying Amy Chapman knew someone who saw Phoebe three times in the woods. *A single instance could be chance, but three implies a deliberate pursuit. That person might be Amos Whitfield*, she thought. *It's a long shot, but it's a place to start.*

Finally, her mind gave in to the fatigue. She leaned over, losing herself in the flickering flames. Her mind drifted to the frothy stream where the faces of Whitfield's victims had spoken to her.

A heavy sadness came when she thought of the conversation she'd been avoiding with Amber. Her daughter had always been precious, yet Maddy's troubles had driven her away. *I can't allow it to continue as is. Tomorrow, I'll call her.*

She pulled a throw blanket from the back of the sofa, covered herself, and fell asleep.

CHAPTER TWENTY-TWO

Zep

Saturday morning, Zep sat with his wife at the kitchen table. Susan read the morning paper while he gazed out the window. She lowered the newspaper and asked what was bothering him.

"I'm worried about Maddy. She's in an awful situation. Adam is away recuperating from surgery. Whitfield came to her house and shot her. The wound wasn't serious, but when she came home from the hospital, he was hiding in her basement, waiting to finish the job. He ended up killing the sheriff who had accompanied her home." He paused and said, "I think the lawn can wait one more day, don't you?"

Susan laughed. "Sure," she said. He reached over, put his hand on hers, and smiled.

"Tomorrow, I'll cut the grass, promise."

He was on his way to Berry Lake by 9:30. On the mountain roads, he thought of how Maddy entered his life. She was in her mid-twenties and had been working the streets with the Utica Police. Zep had just started working for the sheriff's department to tighten the operation.

He was determined to change the department's tradition of no female detectives. Monitoring the performance of women officers in the Utica police from afar, he identified Maddy Reynolds as, hands down, the shining star. He timed his move perfectly. He went to his boss and insisted they bring Reynolds on as the first woman in the

Oneida County Sheriff's Office. His credibility was off the charts, and the wigs gave him what he wanted.

Forty-five minutes after he started, the mountains appeared, and he opened the driver's window to breathe the pristine air. Its herbal scent felt like drinking cool water on a hot day. Putting the Dodge into cruise control, with no cars in front nor behind, Zep leaned back and started reminiscing. He thought of the day he assigned Maddy to her first case. It was a Saturday, an eleven-year-old girl had gone missing, and he gave the case to his star new detective. He expected a run-of-the-mill runaway case, where the kid shows up in a few days, but it was Maddy's introduction to psychopathic killers. Cupid left a trail of dead children, and although Maddy stopped him, it was the beginning of her trail of woes.

It was approaching 11:30 as Zep entered the village of Berry Lake. He remembered the day Maddy gave her termination notice. She was recovering from a gunshot wound from a shootout with the Donnelly gang. Sadly, she had said, "I'm burned out, Zep. I want to move near nature and live in peace."

Unfortunately, your dream didn't come true, Maddy. He crawled through the quaint town, remembering the night The Glades burned and the hell Maddy had endured. Avery Jordan kidnapped her and held her captive, and she barely escaped the fire.

Zep found the road to Maddy's place. Reaching the top of the hill, he stepped out, thought he heard gunshots, and saw Maddy shooting at a target behind the house. Amazed, he watched as she nailed the inner target circles from a hundred yards. When she finished and removed her ear covers, he said, "Not bad."

"Zep, what are you doing here? Don't scare me like that."

"It was too nice a day to cut the lawn, so I thought I'd visit with you." Wiping the sweat from her face with the towel that hung from her neck, she gestured to the house.

"Come inside where it's cool." Zep gazed at the surrounding mountains and the Lake view from her house.

"It's incredible," he said.

"It's a lot nicer when there are no serial killers or sex traffickers around," Maddy quipped. She asked him to get comfortable.

"I've got lemonade, beer, and ice water."

"Lemonade sounds good," he said. She brought two glasses to the living room, handed him one, and sat.

"How are the injuries?" he asked.

She looked at the bandage on her arm. "It's healing well. The headaches come and go but are fewer."

"I see your shooting skills are back," Zep said.

"Yeah, it's funny what you don't do when you're happy." She laughed.

"So, where are you at, Maddy?" She looked at him and asked what he meant. "Are you looking to take him out?"

She looked to the side. "Yes, I am."

"I won't preach at you, but revenge is a two-edged sword. Be careful with it. It can damage the victor as much as the vanquished."

"I just can't get the image of Sheriff Collins lying on my basement floor out of my mind or Beverly Arnold's sweet smile before I left her. I know it's wrong to take a life out of revenge. The night I thought the guy killed Adam, I almost did it. Thank God you and Hannah talked me out of it. My life would be unimaginable if I had killed him. Yet, Whitfield seems different. Maybe it's that he enjoys killing too much. He's just like Cupid, preying on the innocent and vulnerable. He wants to kill Phoebe Hicks. For God's sake, she's a nine-year-old girl!"

"I killed a man I didn't have to," Zep said. "We had discovered the mutilated remains of three of my men, and we caught the enemy soldier who did it. I pulled the trigger and didn't feel bad. I didn't feel remorse. I felt nothing, and that's what eventually got to me. That cold numbness: it's not human to feel that way. It took a long time to recover. Susan helped me. I'd hate to see you go through that, Maddy."

"If you are in a battle with Whitfield, kill him without hesitation, but don't make eliminating him your mission." He shook his head. "I said I wouldn't preach, but here I am."

Maddy smiled. "Your words matter to me. They always have."

She asked if he was hungry, and he said he was famished. "Let's hit Lena's for lunch," she said. He wondered what Lena's was. "That's right, I forgot. You've never been to Berry Lake before. It's the only diner around and thank God the food is good."

They climbed into Maddy's Jeep and headed for town. "I can't believe how beautiful this area is," he said. "Now I understand why you were so excited about moving here."

They reached Main Street, and Zep saw the banner over the street promoting the town fair. Given the circumstances with Whitfield, he inquired if the event was still taking place. She said it was. "Oh, that's not a good idea," he said, shaking his head.

They entered Lena's and grabbed a booth, and Maddy looked for Rose, but she wasn't there. Emma, a fragile-looking older woman who filled in sometimes, came to the table. Maddy asked where Rose was.

"She'll be working a long shift on the day of the town fair, so they gave her today off. What will you have?" After they placed their orders, Zep asked how Adam was progressing.

"Adam is doing well, but I'm not confident how well we are doing."

"What do you mean?"

"I've been mentally elsewhere since the Whitfield situation. I feel very disconnected from him. We talk on the phone, and I visit him, but sometimes we're worlds apart."

"You two seem to have a strong enough foundation that you should be okay."

"That's what Adam says when we talk about it."

Emma brought the food, and they became silent as they ate. During the meal, Zep paused, placed his cheeseburger on the plate, and looked at Maddy, wanting to speak. She gazed at him.

"We both know Whitfield is on a collision course with you. This guy has killed many. He's even taken down a few cops. He thinks he's bigger than life, and that's his weakness. If given the chance, he'll overplay his hand. Let him. He's most vulnerable when he thinks you're scared, and that's when to make your move."

They finished at Lena's and were driving back, and Zep said he wished he could help her. "I have everything you've taught me right here." She pointed at her head and smiled.

Zep looked at Maddy, smiling, thinking she always faced her perils alone and without complaining. It made her courageous, but he thought Maddy must experience profound loneliness. She opened up to him but never crossed that line. Although Maddy was somewhere between a daughter and a friend, she always fiercely guarded the loneliness he knew she hid.

They spent the afternoon on the deck, sipping lemonade and discussing their families, old times, and plans for the future. He told her he was buying a fishing boat to lose himself on summer afternoons. "I tried golfing, but it's just not me. Sitting in a boat with Bud or Al and an ice chest of cold Utica Club is much more my style."

"What about the fish?" Maddy asked.

"Oh, yeah, the fish. I enjoy catching the fish, too." Maddy laughed.

"Do Adam and you have plans when he comes home?"

"We plan to visit my grandkids out west and possibly stop at the Grand Canyon on the way back."

"The Grand Canyon?" Zep said.

"You know that big hole in the earth? The one everyone talks about," Maddy said, laughing.

"I never took you as a Grand Canyon kind of person."

"I don't want to know what you took me as," she said with a smile.

"You're right," he said. "All I've ever known about you is your work as a cop."

She looked at him with sadness on her face. "That's because it's all I've ever accomplished."

Zep realized he'd hit a soft spot. "There are people grateful for what you've done." He sighed. "You deserve your trip out West to see your grandkids and the Grand Canyon. Hell, to the moon if you want." Zep glanced over, and Maddy crossed her arms with tears. He had hit that place within her, that impenetrable wall beyond which she had never let him go.

It was time to leave. Zep caught himself gazing at her, wondering if he would see her alive again. Maddy noticed. She reached over and took his hand. It was as if she knew what he was thinking. "You've been a good coach, Zep. It felt like my dad had reentered my life when I met you." Her smile couldn't take away the sadness he felt.

"You've been a good student," he said. "The best I ever had." A cloud covered the sun, and a crow cawed in the distance. They remained in the moment until he said he should be going.

As Maddy walked him to his car, Zep said if she needed anything, she could call him. "Anything, even to just talk. I mean it." They reached his Dodge and turned to each other.

He had said all he could. He put out his arms and held her. As he turned to open the car door, he stopped. "Wait, I almost forgot." He fished out a small piece of plastic from his wallet, opened it, pulled out a tiny religious medal, and held it in the palm of his hand.

"It's Saint Michael. He's the patron saint of warriors. My mother gave it to me before I went to Nam. It's a bit worn because it's seen a lot of use." He moved his hand toward her and said he wanted her to have it. "Keep it close by. Saint Michael is the angel who fought against Satan in Heaven and cast him into hell. If you go up against Whitfield, send the son-of-a-bitch into hell."

Maddy took the medal from his hand and gazed at it. "Thank you, Zep." He got into his car and glanced at her before descending the hill. Thinking of his afternoon with Maddy on the ride home, he realized he loved her. It was hard not to; she was special in so many ways.

Returning to the life he loved, he watched the sun fall as he neared his home. He loved everything: his wife and kids, the job, and even lawn mowing. It was a life he once believed he'd never survive to experience. Thinking of Maddy and how she was being tested as he had been, he realized, unlike him, she was facing the enemy alone and on his terms. He hoped he'd done his job well and had given her what she needed to survive the onslaught of the notorious Amos Whitfield. He knew no one more capable than her to take down the accomplished killer.

As he drove his street, the sky turned red. Two boys tossed a baseball back and forth in the road. Three girls rode tricycles in a driveway, and a couple of older women chatted with one another from their lawns with their arms crossed. Zep thought the evening was delightful. *But it's not that way for Maddy. She has the job of stopping the monsters at the gate.*

CHAPTER TWENTY-THREE

Marjorie

Two days tuned into two weeks. What had started as an infatuation developed into a full-blown love affair, and Marjorie and Lester wanted to keep Phoebe's presence a secret. She figured as long as the girl was safe and happy, she was okay with it.

Marjorie sat at the kitchen table making a grocery list when Phoebe burst through the back door. Her flame-colored hair flowed behind her, and with her face lit up like a Christmas tree, she said, "Look what I found in the barn! Lester said I can keep it!" She held a white miniature rocking horse made of soapstone. "I'm going to name her Ginger after my kitty." She handed it over, and Marjorie lifted it.

"It's so heavy," she said. Lester stood in the doorway, smiling.

"It was in that chest filled with old odds and ends," he said. "Phoebe picked it out."

"I'll put it in my room," Phoebe said, taking it back. They had fixed up the spare bedroom as Phoebe wanted, and it became hers. Lester stood with his hands in his pockets as she bolted out of the kitchen.

"She sure is a pistol," he said.

"I have a grocery list," Marjorie said. "Will you stop at the store, Lester? We need a few things. I'm making a pot roast for dinner."

"When I finish in the barn, I'll go," he said. Marjorie completed her list and sat next to Phoebe on the sofa while she watched cartoons. She grabbed a *Good Housekeeping* magazine from the coffee table and began flipping through the pages. She couldn't believe how having a child in her house had lifted her spirits.

An article discussing decorating a girl's bedroom caught her attention, and although something inside told her not to do it, she started reading. Before she knew it, she made notes beside bedspread photos and jotted wall color ideas that might coordinate.

Lester came in, and she closed the magazine. "I'm heading to the store now." She picked up the list from the coffee table and handed it to him. Phoebe asked him to get her Eggos.

"Would you like me to write it on the list?" Marjorie asked.

"Nah, I'll remember."

When he walked out, something lingering for days in Marjorie worked at her insides. Each time it resurfaced, she had dismissed it, but not now. *Who am I kidding? This won't last.*

She began feeling foolish in her self-deception and put her head in her hands as the charade she and Lester had concocted came crashing in on her. *I'm just an old, childless fuddy-duddy.* She began crying and retreated to the kitchen to avoid Phoebe's gaze. Lester came in with bags of groceries and gave her a concerned look.

"What is it, Marj?" She shook her head with a napkin to her face and couldn't speak. He sat beside her and put his hand on her arm. "Did something happen?"

"Oh, Lester, we're just kidding ourselves. Eventually, the authorities will find out about Phoebe and take her." Lester appeared gut-shot and looked at the floor.

"You're right," he said. He turned and folded his hands on the table. "What are we going to do?"

"We need to talk with someone we trust and ask for advice."

Simultaneously, they said, "Maddy Reynolds."

Dinner was ready, but Phoebe had fallen asleep in her room, and Marjorie let her be. She returned to the kitchen, where Lester waited. Halfway through the meal, Marjorie asked, "Would you be willing to adopt Phoebe?" She couldn't believe the words had come from her mouth. Lester lay his knife and fork on the table and looked at her, confused.

"Why, I don't know. Would they let us? I mean, we're not exactly young."

"If they care about what's best for her, they would," Marjorie said emphatically. "We love her, and she loves us."

"Can you imagine that?" he said, smiling. "Can you see us at a PTA meeting? That would give people something to talk about, wouldn't it, Marj?"

"I want to, Lester. I want to with all my heart."

"We have to try," he said. "This is our last hope to have a family. Let's discuss this with Maddy."

When they finished, Lester returned to the barn as Marjorie cleaned up, thinking of being Phoebe's mother. She went to the living room and searched for Maddy's number.

"Hi, Maddy, it's Marjorie Best. Would you stop by tomorrow? There's something I'd like to discuss."

"Sure, is everything okay?" Maddy asked.

"Everything is fine; I'll explain when we meet."

She hung up, feeling the emptiness she had lived with for years. Yet, a new excitement of being a mother grew. She checked on Phoebe, and the girl lay on the bed with her eyes open. Sitting beside her, Marjorie said, "You must have been tired. You slept through dinner. Are you feeling okay?"

"Ginger and I are just resting."

"Do you want to bring her to the kitchen? The pot roast is still warm."

"Are you hungry, Ginger?" the child asked the soapstone rocking horse. "She says she's a little hungry," Phoebe told Marjorie. Swinging her legs out from under the covers, she brought Ginger to the kitchen and sat with the keepsake on the table next to her. Marjorie brought a plate with the food.

As Phoebe talked to her imaginary friend, Marjorie waited for the right moment. "Do you like being here with Lester and me?" From the child's expression, Phoebe understood the question held a deeper meaning.

"I love you and Lester," she said.

Marjorie didn't want to get the child's hopes up regarding being adopted. "We love you, too."

"We're full, right, Ginger? Where is Lester?" she asked.

"He's out in the barn."

"Come, Ginger. Let's find more things in the barn." She ran out the kitchen door, and Marjorie sat with her head spinning.

•　　　•　　　•

Lester left for work the following day, and Marjorie sat sipping tea. She was contemplating her upcoming discussion with Maddy. She wasn't wholly positive Maddy wouldn't tell the FBI that Phoebe was at her home, and her stomach felt jittery.

When Phoebe finished her breakfast, she and Marjorie settled in the living room as the girl watched cartoons. Marjorie mended a hole in a sock. There was a knock at the door.

"That must be Maddy," Marjorie said.

Maddy stepped inside, saw the child, and shouted, "Phoebe!" Phoebe ran to her, burying her head in her chest. "I can't believe it's you." Gazing at Marjorie, she said, "How did you find her?"

"Phoebe more or less found me. Come in, Maddy. Let's get comfortable."

Phoebe sat on the sofa beside Marjorie, and Maddy sat across from them.

"Tell me what happened," Maddy said.

"I went outside to cut rhubarb for a pie and noticed the barn door ajar. I had carried Lester's shotgun out, just in case, and stepped inside, holding it, and I found Phoebe in the horse stall."

"Yeah, and I thought she was going to shoot me," Phoebe piped in excitedly, her hands animated and hair flopping wildly. "I said, 'Don't shoot me,' and ran into the woods."

"I want to talk about Phoebe," Marjorie said. She reached her arm around the child and pulled her close. "Can you go to your room with Ginger while Maddy and I talk?"

Phoebe got up, went to Maddy, and wrapped her arms around her. "I'm glad you're better. I saw that man shoot you."

"Thank you for helping me," Maddy said. Phoebe went to her room.

"We've had her here for about two weeks," Marjorie said. "It hasn't been easy hiding her with the FBI and sheriff's cars parked out front. Lester and I love her and think she loves us, too. Maddy, we want to adopt her. Do you think they'll let us? She has no family. Her mother is gone, her father died in the fire at The Glades, and now her grandmother is dead. She has no one."

"I think it's a perfect match," Maddy said. "But the current situation complicates things. I take it you don't want to tell the FBI she's here?"

"No, I don't. They'll put her in a foster home. I don't think they'd let us have temporary custody with the killer on the loose. Do you?"

"No, probably not. Are you worried he'll return here?

"Yes," Marjorie said. "Hannah Bates told me he might have a fixation on me because I inflicted some kind of emotional wound, and he will probably come back."

"That puts Phoebe in harm's way, doesn't it?"

"Yes, I know, but if I turn her over to the authorities, she'll never trust me again. I don't know what to do." Marjorie put her head in her hands, and Maddy sighed.

"Maybe you and Lester should discuss it further. As far as adopting Phoebe is concerned, I think it could happen. But remember that the judge and Child Protective Services will assess your judgment concerning the child's safety."

The phone rang, and Marjorie said she'd be right back. When she returned, she said, "That was Julie Barnes. She reminded me that Friday, she's picking up the blueberry pies I'm making for the town fair."

"Is Amy Chapman working in the booth?" Maddy asked.

"Yes, why?"

"There's something I want to ask her. Can I bring your pies?"

"Sure. It will simplify Julie's to-do list."

Maddy stood. "I'm sure you and Lester will do the right thing. Get creative and ask Hannah if you and Phoebe can go to a temporary safe house together."

"Do you think that's possible?"

"Hannah Bates is a reasonable person. If you cooperate with her, something will get worked out."

"Thanks, Maddy."

"Tell Phoebe I said goodbye," Maddy said.

CHAPTER TWENTY-FOUR

Hannah

It was the morning of the town fair, and agents gathered around a table in the command center for a briefing.

"Are we ready?" Hannah asked Brian.

"We'll have ten agents incognito dispersed throughout the crowd and a team nearby waiting to respond. We have two spotters, one on top of the grocery store, about forty yards away. One's on the dry cleaners' roof." He pointed out the buildings on a map of the village. "The parade will proceed here, down Main Street, and end in the field at the end of town, near the concession stands and rides. The parade starts at nine AM, and festivities run up to the fireworks at dark."

"It's going to be a damn long day," Hannah said. "Remember, everyone, our goal is to prevent Whitfield from subjugating a victim. We need to watch for a man walking too closely with a woman. Questions?"

One of the younger agents hesitantly raised his hand. "What level of force are we allowed to use?"

"Standard FBI protocol." Hannah rattled off the regulation as if she'd said it a thousand times. She read it because she had to, but she knew Whitfield would never allow himself to be taken alive. "Let's remember whom we're dealing with here, people. This guy will kill the victim and you without batting an eye, so let's be extra cautious. Pass this on to your teams. Is there anything else?"

"Should we home in on someone who looks like Ernie Bajorek?" Sara asked.

"No, no, no!" Hannah said. "We cannot confirm if Bajorek is Whitfield. And if he is Amos Whitfield, you won't recognize him because he's a master of disguise. We keep our eyes open for anyone and anything unusual. If that's it, let's get moving."

Hannah drove alone to the village, wanting to gauge the size of the crowd gathered on the street. It was 7:45 when she arrived at Lena's diner, and when she got out, the sun was peeking over the mountains, and it was getting hot. She stepped inside, and people packed the restaurant.

Don't these people realize there's a serial killer on the loose? She searched for a seat when Rose approached.

"Hang on," she said. "I'll clean a table for you." Rose finished and waved Hannah to a spot next to a window overlooking the street.

"This place looks packed," Hannah said.

Rose rummaged for a pen in her pocket. "There are more people than normal. I don't recognize most of them. I think the town did a lot of promotion outside the area this year."

Hannah ordered coffee and a toasted bagel, thinking the day could be a nightmare. She saw cars lining up and people searching for spots to view the parade. *We don't have enough people.*

Rose brought her food, and Hannah asked if she'd spoken to Maddy recently.

"She stopped by the night Sheriff Collins died at her place," Rose said. "She gave me a ride home and made me promise not to walk home after work. But I haven't seen her since." Hannah nodded. "Things have been awful creepy around here lately," Rose added. "My friends are not out there."

"How late do you have to work?" Hannah asked.

"Right up to the bitter end—midnight."

"I'd take Maddy's advice tonight. Do not walk home alone!" Rose gave her a frightened look before she ran to take an order.

Hannah's cell phone rang, and it was Brian, telling her everyone was in position.

"Are there people along the street?" she asked. He said yes.

"Okay, I'll meet you at the concession stands and rides."

She bit into a bagel. Her stomach was tight, and she didn't finish. Putting money on the table, she looked around at the unsuspecting faces before walking outside to stroll along the street.

Families waited excitedly along the curb; many had kids holding balloons with looks of anticipation on their faces. She felt as if she were Chief Brody in *Jaws*, knowing a hungry shark was waiting for people to enter the water.

Brass horns and a booming bass drum turned all eyes left. A red fire truck gleaming in the sunlight followed the Berry Lake High School marching band. Hannah looked in the opposite direction, eyeballing the body positions of pairs of men and women.

The sun was in her eyes; it was difficult to see as she walked along the sidewalk. She passed by Stanley Hartman's tailor shop and peeked in the window. The place was dark, and clothing was hanging on metal racks waiting for owners. She went by Lester's Hardware Store, and Lester was arranging a display of garden tools in the front window.

Reaching the vendors preparing for hungry people, the smells of popcorn, cotton candy, sausage, chicken, and hot dogs filled the air. She saw Brian, dressed in a green tee shirt, jeans, and sneakers, standing with his arms folded, chatting with a pizza vendor. He walked to her.

"It feels like the calm before the storm," he said.

"People will flood this place after the parade," she said. The sound of a generator starting startled her. Hannah snapped her head. A man was tending the Ferris wheel. *I'm really on edge.*

"There's Maddy Reynolds," Brian said. Maddy appeared unusually preoccupied as she walked in their direction, and Hannah called to her. "I never expected to see you here," she said.

"I brought Marjorie's blueberry pies to the church concession for her. I'm heading out before this place gets crazy."

Hannah asked how she was doing. "I'm hanging in there," Maddy said, watching the crowd streaming in. "It looks like the parade is over; I'm out of here." She turned and rushed to her vehicle.

By noon, people mobbed the place; kids lined up to get on the rides, and crowds hovered around the food and beer concession stands. Hannah meandered through the crowd, eyeballing people and repeating the route several times. There were no trees, just occasional tents, and it felt like a sauna. Finally, the noise, the heat, the dust, and her back screaming at her drove her to the parking area, where she sat in a car and drank bottled water. She wished the day was over, but it was only midday.

When she returned to the craziness and found Brian, she told him to give his team a rotating, thirty-minute rest break. It neared dinner time, and the sun dipped behind a mountain, casting a shadow over everything and providing relief. She had eaten nothing since she took a bite from a bagel at Lena's that morning, and now she was hungry. She went to the food stands, bought a chicken and potato dinner, found a place to sit at a picnic table, and watched the crowd as she ate.

Four more hours, she said to herself when she looked at her watch. She returned to perusing, trying to blend as much as a Black woman walking alone through a crowd in Berry Lake could.

As darkness fell, occasional rumblings of motorcycles drowned out other sounds—a few dozen sleeveless cyclists with tattoos on their arms gathered at the beer tents and food stands. A voice came over Hannah's mobile radio. "There could be something by the funhouse."

Hannah shouldered through the crowd, past the Tilt-a-Whirl and Himalaya ride, and ran to a group of people, including two of her agents. Scott Ellers and Jessica Conner questioned a man. He was around forty, and the woman he was with was around eighteen.

"She's my girlfriend," the guy kept saying. The girl had a deer-in-headlights expression. Hannah stepped into the discussion.

"We'll have a brief conversation with your girlfriend; then you can go," she said. Hannah led the girl away from her boyfriend and asked her name.

"Sophie Pappas. Am I in trouble?"

"No, I just have a few questions." She asked who the man she was with was.

"Spencer," she said meekly.

"Do you know his last name?"

"No."

"How long have you known him?"

The girl's voice quivered. "I just met him today." Noticing an accent, Hannah asked where she was from.

"Greece."

"Greece? You mean the country Greece?"

"Yes, I'm a foreign exchange student." Hannah sighed and shook her head.

"Who are you staying with?"

"I'm staying at the Hendersons. They live in the village and permitted me to walk over. I've been getting bored," the girl said. It frightened Hannah that the girl was at the fair alone with Whitfield on the loose.

"Where did Spencer say he was taking you?"

"He said he'd give me a ride home."

"We'll give you a ride home, dear," Hannah said. Sara was nearby, looking on. She waved her over and asked her to give the girl a ride, then walked back to where Brian questioned Spencer. He handed her the guy's driver's license.

"His name is Spencer Duckworth," Brian said. "He's from Albany, and his parents have a camp on Raquette Lake."

"You don't mind if we call them, do you?" Hannah asked. He didn't object, and she requested Brian to take Spencer to their unit, call the family, and check him out.

As they walked away, three loud bangs shook the ground, and the sky lit up with color. The fireworks show had started. Hannah called the units. "This event is nearly over. Now is the most dangerous time. Be on your toes and keep your eyes open when this thing breaks up."

Her stomach tightened again; she wanted a better view of the crowd and walked to the grocery store's roof, where the spotter used night vision equipment to monitor the crowd.

Explosions reflected on the gazing faces, and Hannah wondered if Whitfield was among them, zeroing in on his prey. The massive crowd made serious surveillance seem impossible.

When the fireworks finale ended, people drifted toward the street. The exit went smoothly, except for drunk cyclists yelling obscenities. The field had emptied, most cars had left the village, and Hannah called her team to regroup at the command center. Her team stood around in dusty clothes and sunburned faces, looking exhausted when she arrived. She asked everyone to huddle around.

"Thank you all for sticking with it today. I hope we're out of the woods, but I know we're not. We will find out if the killer has claimed another victim soon. Rest up. We'll be back at eight in the morning. That's it; goodnight." She walked outside to a picnic table, sat, and called home. Anthony answered.

"Was the fair as bad as you feared?" he asked.

"It's too soon to tell. He might dismember a body right now." Silence followed on the other end of the phone. "Sorry, I didn't mean to say that," she said.

"You're tired and under enormous stress, Hannah. Go easy on yourself."

"I wish I were with you," she said.

"Me too.".

Hannah hung up, went inside, and got ready for bed. She found a cot, and her brain unwound as she lay, resting her head on a pillow. She remembered Maddy Reynolds and the far-off look on her face from earlier. *I wonder what that was all about.*

A junior agent operating the phones awakened Hannah at 2:37 AM. "Sheriff Collins' replacement, Carl Davis, is on the phone for you, and he said it's urgent."

"Tell him I'll be right there." She got dressed in sweat clothes and went to the phone.

"Hello, Carl, it's Hannah."

"We have another missing person. Amy Chapman, an older woman who lives with her brother Peter, didn't return from the fair. Peter called us after midnight, and we visited the home. He gave us some names of Amy's friends, but we found nothing. She's missing."

"I need more detail.?" She couched the phone between her head and neck as she spoke, reached for a notepad and pen, and started writing.

"Amy was working the baked goods booth for the First Congregational Church all day. They sold out at about nine, and she helped pack up before she left at about nine-forty. She only lives a few blocks away. She was walking home alone but never made it."

"We need to search the area, starting at the fairgrounds. I'll organize our people, you do the same, and we'll meet you there in thirty minutes."

Damn it! She sighed, gazing into the darkness. Light flashes flickered in the distance, the wind rustled the trees, and a storm blew in. Hannah's stomach jittered as she and her team sped to the location. Carl Davis waited. The wind picked up, and the thunder grew louder as the lightning flashed.

"Where are your men?" she asked.

"Out there," he pointed to the road. "They're searching the sides of the road along the route to Chapman's house." Hannah saw a half-dozen deputies with flashlights walking along the trenches a hundred yards away.

"Why don't I take a few agents and start from Chapman's home," Brian said. "We'll work to meet up with the sheriff's team."

Hannah nodded, and as Brian began organizing a group, Davis got a call from the searchers on his mobile unit.

"We've got something," the voice said.

They walked toward the flashlights as the wind became fierce and leaves blew off the trees. They neared the shadowy figures, and one of Davis's men popped out from the crowd of law enforcement and said they found a body. His face was pale,

"I think it's Amy Chapman, but it's hard to tell."

He led Bates and Davis to a ravine 30 yards from the road. A single deputy stood with his flashlight shining on the ground. "We tried not to contaminate the crime scene," the guy said.

A heavy woman in her sixties, wearing a yellow dress, lay on her back. A stick propped the woman's mouth open. Hannah winced at the sight of a bloody black hole where her tongue was supposed to be. The gash in the woman's throat said Amos Whitfield did it.

"This is a new look," Hannah remarked. "Whitfield didn't cut open her thoracic cavity. He wanted to keep Amy Chapman from talking by taking her tongue." She asked the sheriff to keep his men back. "I'll call our forensic team in." Back at the vehicles, she spoke with all the law enforcement at the scene. The wind drove the rain sideways, forcing her to shout over its gusts.

"I want to pair a sheriff's deputy with an FBI agent to interview everyone who may have seen Chapman yesterday. The sheriffs' familiarity with the locals will aid us in finding the right people." She looked over at Carl Davis for his approval, and he nodded. "Brian, work with Deputy Davis's men."

CHAPTER TWENTY-FIVE

Maddy's heart thumped against her chest as her legs thrust her up the hill behind her house on her tenth and last lap. She reached the top, put her hands on her knees, and let the sweat trickle from her face. After catching her breath, she returned to begin her weapon routine.

She stood a hundred yards from the target, firing from standing, kneeling, and prone positions. Her favorite position was prone, as it allowed for precise accuracy.

After firing, she stood and checked her results. The weeks of daily practice had paid off. *I'm glad I'm back in shape.* It had been years since Maddy's shooting skills were at the High Master Shooter level, and it felt good.

It was the morning of the town fair, and she went inside to shower before picking up the pies at Marjorie's. She knew she had to discuss Phoebe with the FBI soon. On arrival, she waved to the FBI agent in the car. Marjorie answered the door when she knocked.

"Come in."

"Would you like a cup of coffee? I made it fresh."

"Sure."

"Lester and I have been discussing what to do regarding Phoebe, and we've decided. We want to tell Hannah Bates she's here, but do it our way." She sighed and nervously continued.

"We'll invite Hannah here, and all three of us, Lester, Phoebe, and I, will tell her we will cooperate with the FBI as long as we can stay together. We will make it clear we want to adopt Phoebe. Phoebe can share her thoughts; we'll leave it at that." She added with conviction, "The hope of the afflicted will never perish. Wisdom 9:18." When she said that, a memory jogged loose in Maddy's brain. Her mind drifted, trying to recall what it was, but she couldn't.

"So, what do you think?" Maddy snapped back to the moment.

"I think it's an excellent plan. When do you think you'll speak with Hannah?"

"Today's the town fair, so we thought we'd call her tomorrow."

Maddy put her hand on Marjorie's. "I'll support you and Lester every step of the way." She stood and said she should go, and Marjorie handed her a box with two pies.

She had to detour around Main Street as she headed toward the fair because of the ongoing parade. Reaching the field at the edge of town as people trickled into the food concession stands, she pulled over and parked next to a white Cadillac. Maddy noticed the *Reverend D* custom bumper sticker when she got out.

She carried the box and looked for the Berry Lake First Congregational Church sign among the concessions. She found it between the fried dough and candied apple stands. When Maddy walked over, Amy Chapman sat, smiling.

"Why hello, Maddy," she said.

Reverend Dietrich was talking with a couple, holding a book Maddy thought might be a bible. His nod suggested he'd be prompt.

"These are Marjorie Best's blueberry pies."

"Just in time," Amy said. She took the pies and asked her to hang on as she carefully slipped them into aluminum containers, put the dishes on one another, and handed them back. "Tell Marjorie thank you. And how is the poor thing?"

"She's a strong woman; she'll be fine," Maddy said as she picked up the pie dishes. "Are you available tomorrow? I have something to discuss." Maddy was eager to ask her who had seen Phoebe in the woods three times.

"Oh, sure, anytime," Amy said. "I'll be working at the rectory all day."

Dietrich glanced at Amy and Maddy talking. He broke away from the couple and walked to Maddy. He came out from behind the table and embraced her. She put her arm around his shoulder and, for no apparent reason, felt queasy.

"Are you alright, Maddy? You don't look well."

"I'm fine," she said, but she didn't feel fine. "I'll see you tomorrow, Amy," she said as she walked away. Maddy began feeling overwhelmed with an uneasy feeling. The carnival music, kids screeching on the Tilt-a-Whirl, and vendors shouting for people to come to their booths melded into a cacophony of unpleasant noise.

"Maddy," a voice called, and it was Hannah Bates, standing next to Brian Owens. Walking over, she briefly chatted with the two FBI agents, then continued to her Jeep, shouldering her way through the growing crowd. She reached it, got in, and closed the door. She put her head on the steering wheel. *What the fuck is going on with me? I have to get away from here.*

Driving out to the main drag, she reached Route 3, bolted toward her house, and climbed the road up her hill. Ascending the stairs to the deck, she sat, looking out over the lake, and her heart was pounding. Unable to understand what had caused her to feel so crazy, she realized her unconscious mind had made a connection that her conscious mind had not yet grasped.

Maddy hadn't had a panic attack in years, but now she wondered if she was having one. Taking deep breaths to slow her heart, she finally calmed herself. A slight breeze kicked up, and she watched clouds in the distance coming from the east, moving toward Berry Lake. Sitting back, she closed her eyes, feeling the sensations of the sun and a few clouds playing hide and seek with each other, sending shadows onto her face. She drifted off to sleep.

Something awakened her. Uncertain of what had startled her, she sat on the edge of her chair and looked around. Thinking it was a bad dream, she went to the house. It was only 7:12 in the evening but she gave up on the day and went to her room. Getting into comfortable clothes, she lay on top of the bedcovers with the Glock on the nightstand and let her mind drift into sleep.

•   •   •

Maddy woke up with the wind blowing the curtains and rain spraying her back. She got up, closed the windows, and stood, running her fingers through her hair. It was the middle of the night. She remembered how odd she felt the prior evening as she walked to the kitchen. A storm raged, and she knew she couldn't sleep; she brewed coffee.

Sitting at the table, with her cup steaming, she looked out at the calamity and thought, *Something strange happened to me yesterday.* Her mind replayed its events, searching for what had sent her into an emotional tailspin.

She remembered starting her day at Marjorie's after her workout. *She was excited to tell me she planned on meeting with Hannah about adopting Phoebe. I left with the pies, and after being detoured around the village, I parked next to Reverend Dietrich's white Cadillac. It was hot, loud, and dusty. I walked through the crowd with the pies, looking for the church baked goods stand.*

Amy and I chatted, and I asked her if we could meet the next day. The reverend swiftly left a conversation and walked to me. He hugged me, and I put my arm around him, and something happened.

Confused and frustrated, she stood and started pacing around her place, talking out loud. "What happened when I put my arm around his shoulder that scrambled my brain?" She stopped, put her hands on her hips, and screamed, "I felt a bandage beneath his shirt. What the fuck!" She dropped into a chair and said, "Can it be?"

Maddy's mind flashed back to the night Whitfield came to her home. She fired her weapon and missed, but the round hit the doorjamb. A piece struck the intruder, and he screamed in pain. She saw him reach around to his left shoulder with his right hand as he ran.

Putting her hands to her head as she sat, she thought, *Can Dietrich be Amos Whitfield?* The thought shook her. *Alright, Maddy, calm down. You're overreacting. We're talking of Reverend Dietrich here.*

She thought of the many conversations when he understood and supported her. Rose had told her Dietrich gave inspiring and insightful sermons about forgiveness and hope. *It can't be. Back off, Maddy.*

Lying on the sofa, listening to the wind, she started drifting off again but then jolted wide awake by a recollection. She remembered Marjorie quoting a bible scripture. Wisdom 9:18, she had said. Near the babbling stream, she heard a choir of Whitfield's victims chanting 'Wiz 262425.' *Could that have been a bible verse?*

She got up, remembering Rose had given her a bible as a gift. Maddy, who hadn't read it due to not being religious, searched the cabinet next to the fireplace, but the book wasn't there. *Where else might it be? My bedroom closet!*

She opened the bedroom closet door, and next to the metal box where she kept her weapons and ammunition, she had stacked a pile of books. Pulling them off the shelf, she placed them on the bed and started rummaging.

This is it, she said, holding a red leather book with *The Holy Bible* inscribed in gold letters on its cover. She flipped open the cover and stared at the note Rose had written. *To my dear friend, Maddy. May the truth always set you free. Rose.*

She turned to The Book of Wisdom and looked up Psalm 26, verses 24 and 25. *Enemies disguise themselves with their lips, but in their hearts,*

they harbor deceit. Though their speech is charming, do not believe them,
for seven abominations fill their hearts.

"Oh my God!" she said as she dropped to the edge of the bed, thinking of the voices by the stream. "They were trying to warn me."

CHAPTER TWENTY-SIX

Hannah

Hannah felt overwhelmed, driving back to the command center in the rain. The case was collapsing, and she felt powerless to halt it.

Battered by the driving rain as she ran into the building, she stepped inside, found tissues to wipe her face dry, and called the staff to her.

"This is where we are, people. Whitfield claimed another victim. We have agents working with local law enforcement interviewing. The rest of us must again review the backgrounds of new men to Berry Lake. Pull out our documents, pair up, and find what we missed. This guy is in a killing frenzy and won't stop until someone stops him."

She went to her desk to give Ben Harris an update. When she finished, she began perusing the floor, moving from one table to another with her arms crossed, watching her team at work. She'd ask for updates and occasionally suggested something.

The agents looked exhausted as the morning light appeared, and Hannah asked one to get pots of coffee going and to bring in pastries. Her people poured through documents, made phone calls, and formed small groups to share information.

Feeling time pressure, she grabbed a set of car keys and headed to visit Marjorie Best. *Marjorie has to have more recollection of her attacker.* She'd seen it before. The slightest remembrance could break a case. *Maybe she'd overlooked something because she thought it was insignificant. The smell of his cologne or a mannerism might give away his identity.* She pulled behind a car where one of her men sat.

"I'm going inside," she told the agent.

CHAPTER TWENTY-SEVEN

Marjorie

Marjorie sat at the kitchen table with her tea, watching the rain pounding the back lawn. The sounds of cartoons and Phoebe's laughter drifted in from the living room. She pondered what she and Lester might say to Hannah Bates when Lester came home for lunch. They planned on calling her together. Startled by a knock, she rushed to the living room, and Hannah Bates stood outside the front door.

"Go to the kitchen, Phoebe," she said.

Marjorie felt her heart beating as she went to let Hannah in. Sweat beaded on her forehead, and she felt warm around her neck. She took a deep breath, tried composing herself, and opened the door.

"Can I come in?" Hannah asked. Marjorie stepped back, and Hannah walked inside, tilting her head. "Is there something you want to tell me?"

"Lester and I were going to call and tell you about Phoebe when he gets home at noon," she said.

"How long has she been here?" Hannah asked. Marjorie's mind was on Phoebe, listening from the kitchen.

"Almost two weeks. We want to adopt her, Ms. Bates. Lester and I love her and want to be with her wherever you place her."

"Can we sit?" Hannah asked. They walked in and sat. Hannah folded her hands on her knees and took a deep breath as if trying to calm herself before saying something difficult.

"I'm sure you and Lester will make wonderful parents. But the killer wants you and the child dead. He is killing at a rapid pace, and last night, he killed Amy Chapman."

"Oh, my Lord, Amy Chapman?"

"He's in a frenzy and will keep killing," Hannah said. "We have to take the girl today. We must also increase security around your place; one vehicle out front is insufficient."

"Can Lester and I join Phoebe?"

"It may take a few days to clear with the family court judge and CPS. We'll work it out. In the meantime, we need to keep you both safe. You'll need to get Phoebe's things together, and I'll have Angela, our social worker, and an agent here at noon to get her."

Bates stood and started for the door, and Marjorie followed. Before stepping into the rain, Hannah turned. "I'll support you and Lester through the adoption process. But please understand what I am doing today is for everyone's safety while we address the current threat."

That didn't go as planned, Marjorie thought. *But it's not all bad. In a few days, we'll be able to be with Phoebe.* She walked to the kitchen, wondering how much Phoebe had heard and how she'd react. She stopped at the doorway, and the girl was gone.

Torrential rain slapped Marjorie in the face when she ran outside screaming, "Phoebe, come back!" She ran into the woods, following a streak of yellow, yelling, "Phoebe, Phoebe, please wait!" The constant crashing of water muffled her voice.

Soaked-through house slippers felt like weights on her feet. Out of breath, she held her side and leaned against a tree as water dripped into her eyes. Pushing off, she kept moving, dragging her feet, holding onto trees, stepping over fallen tree branches, and occasionally stumbling on a rock.

Phoebe's yellow shirt drifted in and out of sight. Marjorie kept moving toward where she thought she saw her last as her body trembled. The temperature cooled, and the woods seemed to continue forever. She always took caution to avoid getting lost by not venturing too far.

Aimlessly, she moved forward for almost an hour until she saw Phoebe climbing a distant hill across a stream. She yelled to her. The girl stopped and looked in her direction. "Please wait for me, Phoebe; I won't let them take you!" The child continued running, undeterred. Halfway down the slope, Marjorie slipped, fell on her back, and slid into the swiftly rushing stream, screaming. Her right ankle felt as if someone had put a torch to it, and the burning pain ran up her lower leg as she screeched. She sat up in the water, placed her hands over her ankle, and saw blood oozing from her pant leg.

Using her hands, she pushed herself forward on her rump out of the freezing water, then squirmed halfway up the hill. She collapsed, put her head on her forearm, and wept. The only sound was the loud rain pounding the ground. Feeling helpless, she lifted her head, wondering what she'd do. She looked up and saw Phoebe standing nearby with her eyes wide and tears streaming down her cheeks, mixing with the rain.

"You're bleeding," the child wept. "Does it hurt?" Marjorie sat up, put her arms out, and the girl ran to her, falling into her embrace. They clung to one another, and Marjorie kept kissing her face as they cried.

"I thought I lost you," Marjorie said.

"I didn't think you'd come after me."

She asked the child to help her stand, and together, they hobbled to the top of the hill. She stopped and leaned against a tree. "I don't know my way out of these woods."

"I do," Phoebe said. "I know where I am. This stream leads to a field near Aunt Betsy's house; we sometimes walked here."

"How far is it?"

"Not too far. I know the way."

"Hand me that broken tree limb, and I'll use it as a crutch," Marjorie said, propping herself. They plodded through the pounding rain and over uneven ground, occasionally stopping to rest. Marjorie's ankle and lower leg throbbed.

Reaching an open space, Phoebe shouted through the noise, "This is Aunt Betsy's field!" Their feet sloshed as they crossed the soaking meadow. Marjorie's body was numb, and the only other sensation was her lower right leg pulsing. A Victorian house emerged from the fog at the end of the field.

"This way," Phoebe said. She headed to a back door. Before reaching it, she stopped, walked to a small concrete figurine of a naked cherub, leaned it to the side, and grinned as she held up a hidden key. She unlocked the door, and they entered a coat room. It was dismal, gray, and cold. Phoebe flipped a switch, and a dull light lit the room.

I need to change out of these clothes. Marjorie felt feverish and numbness in her lower leg and said, "I'm freezing. Are there clothes or blankets in here?"

Phoebe pointed to a stairway, and they climbed together, leaning on one another. They reached the top and started down a hallway. Phoebe opened a door, and they stepped into a bedroom. "This is Aunt Betsy's room." Opening a dresser drawer, Marjorie shuffled through night clothes until she picked out the warmest she could find. She put them on and hung her wet clothes over a cold radiator.

"I need to get warm." She walked to the bed, pulled back the covers, and laid her body on the sheet.

"Look at your leg," Phoebe said, pointing to the swollen shin with a gouge oozing red pus.

"Find me a wet washcloth, please." Phoebe left her and returned with a partially wet towel. Patting the wound, Marjorie tried to clean out tiny pieces of the tree branch that had caused the injury.

"Lie down," Phoebe said, opening a blanket and tossing it over Marjorie. "This should make you warm."

Shivering with fever, Marjorie lay on her side as the gray light of midafternoon shimmered outside of a window. Rain pounded against the house, and the wind whistled through cracks in its exterior. Her mind drifted, and a warm body cuddled up to her. Phoebe put her arm around her, squeezed, and held her tightly until she fell asleep.

Shoving Marjorie's shoulder until she opened her eyes, Phoebe whispered, "I heard something." Marjorie's head ached; she listened but heard only the steady rain on the window.

"I know I heard something," Phoebe said. "There, did you hear that?"

"I'm not sure." A loud clunk came from downstairs, and Phoebe asked if she heard it. Marjorie sat.

"Yes, I heard it. Who do you think it could be?"

"Maybe it's Aunt Betsy."

"Would she come here late at night?"

"I don't know," Phoebe said as she slipped out of bed. Marjorie asked where she was going.

"I'm going to look outside." The girl walked to the window and pulled back the curtains.

"It's not her car," she said. "I see a man; he's carrying something."

Marjorie put her feet on the floor, her head spun, and she had to steady herself. "Help me make this bed," she said. "We better hide." Phoebe went to the opposite side and helped arrange the covers.

"Can you fit under the bed?" Marjorie asked.

"I think so."

"I'll hide in the closet; you crawl under there and stay perfectly still," Marjorie said. Phoebe helped her hobble to the closet and shut the door, and Marjorie shivered as she waited in the dark.

A door closed somewhere in the house, and footsteps on the stairs sounded far away. The guy was entering the basement. Time passed, and as Marjorie waited, she put her hand on her wound; it felt hot and probably infected.

Maybe he's gone, she thought, but no sooner than the thought hit her, footsteps sounded on the stairs to the bedrooms. They got louder, and she stiffened. The floor creaked; he was in the hall. A door opened, and a switch clicked. Light streamed beneath the closet door. *Oh, my God, he's in the room.*

The doorknob rattled, the closet door slowly opened, and a flashlight blinded her. The flashlight switched off, and a man held a gun, smiling.

"Reverend Dietrich?"

CHAPTER TWENTY-EIGHT

Hannah

Sara anxiously awaited as Hannah arranged for Phoebe's placement with Child Protective Services over the phone. When she hung up, Sara said, "We've been calling the Best home to arrange picking up Phoebe Hicks, but there's been no answer. Our guy finally went inside, and the house was empty."

"Have you tried calling Lester at the hardware store?"

"Brian's talking with him right now." Hannah walked to where Brian stood and waited until he hung up the phone.

"Lester doesn't know what happened to his wife and the girl," he said. "They were home when he left."

"All right," Hannah said. "Get a team together, including Larry and some of his people, and meet me here in five minutes." While getting rain gear from the back room, she found a note from Sara on her pillow that her husband called. She was missing him.

Two carloads of agents, including Larry Simmons and three of his people, started through the rain to the Best home. Hannah's cell phone rang, and her boss returned her call.

"Whitfield claimed another victim in Berry Lake last night."

"Who was it?"

"Her name was Amy Chapman. She was in her sixties and was working a concession stand at the town fair. He took her tongue." She heard Harris sigh. "That's not all. Marjorie Best and Phoebe Hicks are missing."

"I thought we had someone watching the home."

"We do. We're on our way," she said.

When Hannah and her team arrived, Lester sat on a sofa holding his head, and the FBI agent from the car out front sat next to him. Hannah sat as the other agents spread throughout the house.

"What can you tell me, Lester?"

"I left here this morning at about six-forty-five for the hardware store. Marj and I were going to call you at noon and tell you we wanted to adopt Phoebe. While at work, I received a call from one of your agents claiming no one answered at my home. I quickly locked up and got here as fast as I could. The house was empty."

The agent who guarded the front, Joe Tyler, said he had seen no one from the car. "I think he came in from the back."

"Marjorie kept a shotgun in the broom closet," Lester said. "It's still here."

"Whatever happened quickly," Hannah said. Brian returned to the room from the back of the house.

"The foliage in the woods looks like someone had passed through recently. The rain has washed out any markings beyond thirty yards, and it will be impossible to track them. We'll need a search party to find them."

Hannah said the weather prevented a helicopter search. "How far do these woods extend before a public road?" she asked.

"Twenty-five miles back, ten miles west, and about the same to the east," Lester said.

"Is Marjorie familiar with the area behind your house?"

"She deeply fears the forest from getting lost as a kid. No, she's not familiar at all."

"We need to assemble a search party," Hannah said. "Can you contact the fire department and ask for volunteers?" she asked Sheriff Davis. "I can provide a few agents for the search," she said, "but I need the rest at the command center."

It was mid-afternoon when Hannah assembled her people in the school cafeteria.

"Okay, everyone, here's another update on where we are. Someone may have abducted Marjorie Best and Phoebe Hicks into the woods behind the Best home. The sheriffs and local volunteers are searching, including some of our people. The rest of us must put a full-court press on our research efforts. That's all." *I keep repeating the same message to them over and over. I wonder what they must think.*

It was nearly 3:30 in the afternoon. Brian stayed to oversee efforts at the command center as Hannah returned to the Best home to check on the search.

CHAPTER TWENTY-NINE

Maddy

Rocked by the thought that Reverend Dietrich might be Amos Whitfield, Maddy needed a reality check. She waited until 9:00 and called Sidney Myers.

"Sidney, it's me."

"What is it, Maddy?"

"I suspect a man of being Whitfield, but I have no proof; it's strictly intuition. I'm calling so you'll bring me to my senses," she said.

"Your intuition has always been damn good. Tell me more."

"Whitfield came to my home one night, and we exchanged gunfire. My round hit a doorjamb, and a piece of shrapnel struck him in his left upper shoulder. I saw a man yesterday whom I thought I knew well. We hugged, and I felt a bandage in the same spot when I put my arm around him."

"What role is he in?" Sidney asked.

"He's the reverend at the local church. His name is Niles Dietrich, and he moved here from Dayton, where he was a minister. He supposedly has a wife doing missionary work in Africa."

"That's a perfect role for Whitfield," he said. "He's trusted and can move among many circles in a wide region. Do you know if the FBI is investigating him?"

"I'm sure they have. Hannah checked all new males in the area. They must have cleared him."

"Remember, Whitfield is an expert at covering his tracks and assuming false identities," he said. "Having a wife is a perfect cover for a serial killer. He probably told people in his congregation about his wife's letters and how she can't wait to meet everyone; all the while, the real reverend's wife is dead in a swamp, and her husband is in a shallow grave somewhere between Dayton and Berry Lake."

"I get it," she said. "All Whitfield had to do was contact the people expecting Dietrich's wife in Africa and say she succumbed to an unexpected illness, and he's home free."

"Exactly!" Maddy asked why the FBI hadn't detected it.

"Because they likely sent an agent to the church in Dayton to check out Dietrich's story, and it added up. An FBI agent probably showed them a recent headshot photo of the reverend in Berry Lake. Whitfield can look like anybody. The Dayton people thought it was him. Voilà—he's off the shortlist."

"I'm hesitant to bring this to Hannah Bates because it's speculative and not backed up with hard evidence," she said. Sidney said he agreed and asked what she'd do.

"I want to identify at least two victims with a common thread connecting them to the reverend. I'll take it to the FBI. Hopefully, they'll take action."

"That won't be easy," Sidney said. "As a minister, he meets many people during his Sunday services. The connections to Dietrich you're talking about must be unique. They can't be his ordinary interactions with his congregation. You'll need to be careful. Whitfield has a strong survival instinct and will strike first if he senses you're going after him."

"Sidney, he's already struck first."

"Be careful! I'm here if you need me."

Maddy headed into Lenas when it neared the evening, hoping Rose might be working. She wanted to learn as much about Dietrich as possible and hoped Rose, a church member, could give more information.

The rain had receded to a steady drizzle, leaving the streets wet, dismal, and vacant. The somber atmosphere in the diner reminded Maddy of a funeral parlor. Rose came over and sat across from her, looking pale and fearful.

"What's happening here?" Maddy asked. "Where is everyone?"

"There's been another murder, maybe three." Maddy stiffened as she awaited the explanation. "They found Amy Chapman with her throat cut and tongue missing last night." Rose pulled out a pack of Lucky Strike cigarettes with her hand trembling.

"I didn't know you smoked."

"I haven't in years. But now I need something. Marjorie Best and Phoebe Hicks are missing, too. Half the town is searching for them in the woods behind Marjorie's house. They think that guy might have taken them."

Stunned, Maddy sat back. "I must go there." She left the diner, rushed to her Jeep, and started for Lester's house with her mind racing. *None of the pieces fit together. How was Whitfield able to murder Amy Chapman and abduct Marjorie and Phoebe in such a short timeframe? He's not Superman, for God's sake.*

Volunteer firefighter's pickup trucks parked everywhere reminded her of the night of the Glades' fire. As she walked to the back, lightning flashed, and a crack of thunder shook the ground. She saw Bates and the new deputy sheriff dressed in rain gear, talking with each other.

"I heard what happened," she said when she approached. "Could Whitfield have taken Phoebe and Marjorie so shortly after killing Amy Chapman?"

Hannah and Carl looked at one another. "We've come to the same conclusion," Hannah said. "Phoebe didn't want to be taken to a foster home and probably ran off. Marjorie likely followed. The girl knew we were coming to get her today."

"How far back has the search gone?" Maddy asked,

"About five miles. But another storm is moving this way; we're bringing everybody in. We can't start using helicopters until this damn weather clears," Hannah said, pulling out a handkerchief and sneezing.

Lester appeared dazed as he walked in with the crowd from the woods. He entered the house, and Maddy followed.

"Hey, Lester," she said as they stood in the kitchen.

"Hi, Maddy," he said sullenly.

"I'm sorry Marjorie and Phoebe are missing," she said. He sadly nodded.

"I hope Whitfield hasn't gotten them."

"They're probably in the woods," she said.

"I hope you're right. Marj must be so scared. She's afraid of the woods." He shook his head, and Maddy put her hand on his forearm.

"At least she has Phoebe," he said, shuffling into the next room. Maddy went to her Jeep and headed home, having done everything she could. Glancing at the darkness descending on the forest and thinking of Marjorie and Phoebe, lost alone in the freezing weather, Maddy felt powerless.

Her thoughts moved to Whitfield as the rain started pounding the windshield. *Rose said the killer cut out Chapman's tongue. Fuck! Dietrich heard me tell Amy I wanted to speak with her. Removing a tongue is symbolic of keeping someone from talking. He must have been afraid she might reveal too much to me. Dietrich must be Whitfield. I've got to connect two seemingly unrelated victims to him and make a case to bring to Hannah.*

Driving back to her place, she thought of everyone Whitfield had killed or attacked since he started his spree, hoping to tie them to Dietrich. Marjorie and Amy Chapman knew him from the church, but she thought that connection would not implicate him. Lake Placid popped into her head. She remembered Rose saying Abigail was from Lake Placid and wondered if there was a connection to Elizabeth Beckman. She turned her Jeep around and started for Lake Placid. *At this moment, I'm relying on a hunch, but it's all I got.* She had no plan, only a gut feeling.

Maddy's mind drifted to Adam during the hour-and-thirty-minute drive. It was as though they were in separate worlds. She didn't know what he was experiencing after recuperating from the surgery.

Wondering if he would realize his goal of walking without a cane, she worried he might struggle to accept a life with a physical disability if he didn't. *What will our lives be like when he returns home?* So much had changed that she feared their relationship might change, too.

She entered the village of Lake Placid; it was late, 11:30, and the shops were closed. She crept to the end of the main street and pulled into an open gas station. A man was standing by a cash register as she entered.

"I'm supposed to be at the Beckman estate but can't locate it. Can you give me directions?" The guy wrote them out and reviewed them to make sure Maddy understood.

She ran to her Jeep and started on a mountain road with no houses until she finally arrived at a gate with a long driveway that led to a three-story brick mansion. Its lit-up landscaping stood out against the night.

Oh, boy, I hope I know what I'm doing. She drove up, parked in the circular driveway, walked to the double oak doors, and rang the bell. The door opened, and an elderly man, tall and robust looking, with blue jeans and a green tee shirt, said hello. "How can I help you?"

"I'm Maddy Reynolds. I'm sorry for the late hour, but I'm dealing with a dangerous situation, and I'd like to talk with someone who knew Elizabeth Beckman well."

"Elizabeth was my sister. I'm Paul Crouse. Come in, Ms. Reynolds." She stepped into the house.

"I'm from Berry Lake, and I'm trying to unravel the identity of your sister's killer. He wants to kill a woman and a child, and I intend to stop him."

Crouse stepped back, snickered, and said, "Well, that's quite an introduction. Are you always this forthright, Ms. Reynolds?"

Maddy looked at the floor and smiled. "Only when I'm uptight."

"Follow me," he said as he led her to a massive room with furniture clustered in different areas. "I just arrived from my ranch in Wyoming. That's where I live. My sister's murder has left me a bit shaken."

"I understand," Maddy said. Crouse gestured to a chair.

"Are you the famous detective?" he asked.

"I used to be a detective, but not anymore."

"You can take the woman out of the detective role, but you can't take the detective out of the woman, I assume."

Maddy laughed. "You're very perceptive, Mr. Crouse."

"Please, call me Paul."

"Only if you call me Maddy." He smiled.

"Maddy, why don't you ask me what you came to ask me?"

"Did Elizabeth know Abigail Hicks?"

"You sure get to the core," he said. "Yes, Betsy knew Abigail. They were very close friends."

Betsy! she thought. *Phoebe's Aunt Betsy had to be Elizabeth Beckman.*

"I believe your sister and Abigail had a common connection to the killer. I think the man the FBI calls Amos Whitfield is Reverend Niles Dietrich from Berry Lake. Why might both know that man?"

Crouse stared off to the side, said nothing momentarily, and then spoke. "My sister and Abigail go way back. They met in grade school and had fallen in love by the time they graduated high school. I was the only one who knew. I was Betsy's older brother, and she always trusted me."

His voice quivered as he spoke. "They lived double lives, creating what society considered acceptable lifestyles to hide their true selves. It made their lives extremely difficult. They married men and had children. It was heartbreaking to watch what they endured."

Crouse sighed, crossed his arms, and said both women held deeply religious convictions. "They struggled with guilt and shame and always felt alienated from the church with its judgmental attitude. Abigail met Dietrich and experienced his acceptance and understanding. She told him about her relationship with Betsy, and he said she was a child of God, no matter what."

He paused, and Maddy remained silent, waiting for him to continue. "Abigail was so excited; she wanted Betsy to meet the reverend. They started meeting regularly with him at our property near

Berry Lake. He made them feel good about themselves. Maybe for the first time.”

“Did your sister ever mention the name Phoebe?”

“Yes, I know about Phoebe.”

“Phoebe is the child I mentioned whom Dietrich wants to kill because he thinks she can identify him.”

“Oh, Jesus,” he said.

“Do you know if Abigail brought Phoebe to the meetings with the reverend?”

“I don’t think so.”

“Phoebe and Marjorie Best, the other woman Dietrich wants to kill, got lost in the woods south of Berry Lake,” Maddy said. “Phoebe told me she knew how to find Aunt Betsy’s place. They may have found their way to your property. They are vulnerable to the killer. Please give me directions to the home.”

He retrieved a piece of paper and two keys from another room. “This key is to the front door. This one is a master that unlocks all the doors inside the house. The place is remote, and the dirt road is difficult to locate. If you follow these directions, you should be okay.” She took the paper and keys, thanked him, and rushed to the door.

“Godspeed, Maddy Reynolds,” he said as he watched her run to her Jeep.

Maddy drove along the winding roads to Berry Lake, convinced Niles Dietrich was Amos Whitfield, and thought it was time to call Bates. She tried dialing the number, but there was no cellular service. She realized she’d have to wait until she was out of the tall peaks surrounding Lake Placid to make a connection.

CHAPTER THIRTY

Hannah

Hannah watched as Deputy Davis pulled the searchers out of the woods. The rain started falling in buckets, and lightning strikes were everywhere. She stayed at the Best home and met with Davis in Lester's kitchen to debrief. They planned the next day's activities and hoped the volunteer firefighters would show up at first light.

She returned to a bustling command center just before midnight.

"How's it going?" she asked Brian.

"We have two agents assigned to each man."

"Okay, I'll be right back." She went to her cot and returned Anthony's call. "Are you still up?"

"More or less," he said, sounding exhausted.

"I'm sorry it took so long to get back to you," she said.

"That's okay. I'm keeping track of how much time you owe me. I'm thinking of a week away on an island without cell phones."

"You won't have to ask me twice," she said.

"I'm not even going to ask what you're dealing with. Just promise you'll come home to me in the same condition you left."

"I can't wait to come home."

"I'm keeping your side of the bed warm," he said.

She looked at the hard cot where she sat. "Don't even talk to me about a bed."

They said they loved each other, and when they hung up, she felt a hollow aching inside and wished the Whitfield ordeal was over so she could return to her family.

She walked to where her team worked and started moving from table to table. The night dragged until 3:30, when two agents raised their hands. Brian inquired what they had.

"I'm not sure," Nick Presley, the senior of the two agents, said. "Here's a photo taken the day Niles Dietrich left Dayton." Hannah was listening. "The man resembles the reverend."

"What's the problem?" she asked.

"Look at the car," Presley said. "He's standing next to a blue Dodge Charger." A group of smiling people held a sign that said *Good luck on your new assignment, Reverend Dietrich!*

"What about it?" Hannah asked. Presley laid another photo on the table.

"This photo was in the church newsletter here in Berry Lake. They took it the day Dietrich arrived in that white 1995 Cadillac a few days later. We checked the National Vehicle Database, and it has no record of a white Cadillac ever being registered to Niles Dietrich."

Hannah carefully compared the two photos of the men, noticing their strong resemblance. "Get Larry Simmons over here," she said. Presley went looking for the forensics team leader.

"Larry, conduct a facial analysis of the two men in the photos to check for similarity," Hannah requested.

"I'll get right on it."

Stepping outside to get air, she watched a second storm blow in. When she returned, Brian looked over two agents, and Hannah listened. Abby Hemstreet, a tech, spoke.

"We looked back at Whitfield's first murder in 1965," the woman said. "It took place in Raleigh, North Carolina. He worked as a clerk in a pharmacy, where he used the name Amos Whitfield for the first time, and it stuck. We also found an anomaly in the medical school roster at Duke University twenty-five miles away that same year."

Abby Hemstreet shuffled through papers on her desk as she spoke. "The semester ended with one less student than it started with. There's no record of anyone dropping out," she said. "We delved deeper and discovered an undisclosed unauthorized modification to the records. The missing student's name was Albert Lynn, from South Dakota. Our handwriting experts determined the student and the pharmacy clerk have identical signatures. The only other time that handwriting shows up is New York State Motor Vehicles three years ago when Niles Dietrich applied for a driver's license."

"Excellent work," Brian said.

Hannah's heart picked up its beat. The new information confirmed the long-held suspicion that Amos Whitfield was a trained physician and drew a direct line to a man in Berry Lake.

She looked over and saw Larry Simmons rushing their way, holding a handful of documents.

"These are different men in the photos," Larry stated. He held a schematic of the two faces with various measurements and comparisons. "They're close, but the Dietrich that left Dayton is not the Dietrich that arrived in Berry Lake."

"Brian, I think we have our man."

Sara called to her, "Maddy Reynolds is on the phone for you." Hannah looked at her watch; it was 4:10 AM, and she wondered what the call could be about. She took the phone.

"Hannah, I visited Elizabeth Beckman's brother, Paul Crouse, tonight in Lake Placid. I left him a couple of hours ago, and he told me Abigail and Elizabeth were lovers. He said they met with Niles Dietrich regularly." There was a pause before Maddy continued.

"He played the understanding pastor's role to the max, got them to trust him, and made them feel accepted. The bastard must be Whitfield. Do you have the grounds to bring Dietrich in for questioning and hold him until we find Marjorie and Phoebe?"

"We'll bring him in immediately," she said.

"Hannah, I am heading to the Crouse family's house outside Berry Lake. It's where Dietrich met with Abigail and Elizabeth. Phoebe knows the place, and I'm hoping I'll find her and Marjorie Best there." Before they hung up, Maddy gave Hannah the address.

"Brian, get two agents. We're going to pay a visit to Reverend Dietrich."

They piled into an unmarked car and arrived at the rectory next to the chapel where Dietrich lived. The place was dark; the driveway was empty. They knocked and rang the doorbell, but there was no answer. Returning to the car, Hannah pulled out the paper with the address of the house outside Berry Lake that Maddy had given her. "Step on it," she told Brian.

CHAPTER THIRTY-ONE

Marjorie

"Well, well, well. What do we have here?" Dietrich said when he found Marjorie huddled in the closet. "Come out of there," he shouted. She struggled to her feet. "What are you doing here?"

"I got lost in the woods during the storm and followed a creek that led me here."

"The Lord works in mysterious ways, doesn't he?" Dietrich said. He sounded as if he were an entirely different person. His voice was harsher, and his smile was wide and appeared cynical, unlike the empathetic smile Marjorie had known.

She couldn't fathom how Reverend Dietrich could be the same person berating her. She stood in the robe and nightshirt and leaned on the wall, keeping her weight off the injured leg. With a smile, he examined her from head to toe. "You better get your undies," he said, gesturing to her underclothes that hung over the radiator. She limped over, put the partially wet clothes over her arm, and walked to where he opened the door.

"Where are you taking me?"

"None of your business, you high and mighty bitch." He shoved her as she walked by, and she fell into the hallway, hitting her head on the railing. A sharp pain piercing her head and blood dripping to the floor shook her to her core, and she began trembling. "You think you're better than everybody." He kicked her ribs, knocking the air from her lungs. She gasped and prayed, *Help me, God.*

"You're not better than me!" Dietrich screamed. "Get up!" he yelled. She started lifting herself. He shouted, "I said move it!" and knocked her to the floor again. Her vision darkened, and she was losing consciousness. "What's wrong, Miss Perfect Body? I see how you hide your tits under all those clothes. Who were you keeping them for, Maynard? Don't think I haven't heard about you and him. Well, he's not getting at them anymore, is he? I took care of him."

The room spun. Marjorie was on the verge of vomiting. "Get up! Get up! Get up!" he screamed. She dragged herself to her knees, then pushed up and leaned on the railing in the hallway. "Now, down the stairs." She gimped along, holding the handrail. The room was still spinning. She started on the steps, he kicked her, and she tumbled to the landing. "You are scum!" he screamed.

Seeing double, she felt blood dripping from the cut on her head into her eyes. Dietrich stepped over her, then dragged her down the stairs the rest of the way by her robe. Disoriented, in agonizing pain, and quaking with fear, Marjorie felt her life slipping away.

Enraged, he said, "I asked you to join my prayer group, but not you! You think you're too good for me. I'll show you how good you are." He pulled her by the hair and dragged her along the hardwood floor to the basement door. Screaming, feeling her hair might pull out of her scalp; the pain was unlike anything she'd ever experienced.

As she lay before the basement stairway, she looked up at the hatred on his face before he pushed her with his foot, sending her tumbling the steps to the floor. Feeling the jab and jolt of each step on her ribs as she rolled to the hard-packed dirt floor, she heard him cry out, "I'll be right back, bitch." The lock on the door clunked shut.

Marjorie was burning with fever and felt like her body was an open sore; everything hurt. The room was chilly, the floor was hard, and she wanted to die. Her last thought before passing out was, *Thank God Phoebe is safe.*

Drifting into a chaotic, disturbing dream, she lay on the chilly, damp dirt floor until breaking glass awakened her. She tried to lift her head and look around, but the pain was too intense, and she rested it on the floor.

"Marjorie, wake up!" She opened her eyes, and Phoebe kneeled, pushing her shoulder.

"Phoebe," Marjorie slurred. She reached out her hand and asked if she was okay. The child took it, held it to her chest, and wept.

"I'm okay," she whimpered, "but you're not." She tried to lift her to a sitting position but lacked the strength. "We need to get you out of here. Help me sit you up." Marjorie lay weak and semiconscious. "Please don't die!" she screamed. The girl pulled at her until she sat up. "Oh, my head. Where did that man go?" Marjorie asked.

"He said he was coming right back. I heard him talking outside a broken window, and I think he went to his car."

"Check if the basement door is unlocked," Marjorie said.

"It's locked; I already tried."

"Then how did you get in?"

"Through the basement window, but I barely fit. He'll be back soon."

Marjorie gathered her strength and firmly said, "You must go."

"No, I'm not leaving you alone."

"If you leave now, you can get help."

Phoebe huffed and wrapped her arms around Marjorie. "I love you," she said.

"Go now and hurry." The child disappeared into the basement's darkness, and Marjorie laid her head back on the floor.

An upstairs door slammed, and her eyes opened. She listened as footsteps above grew louder. A lock clunked again, and a door squeaked open. A man's long shadow stretched over the basement steps. Marjorie attempted to hide in the darkness but could hardly move. Footsteps, one at a time, grew closer, and the shadow got longer.

She heard a deep and raspy voice. "Where do you think you're going?" She looked up. Dietrich's expression had changed. His facial lines were harsher and more defined. He no longer had to pretend.

A satchel hung from one hand and a fold-up table from the other. Dietrich set the satchel on the floor and unfolded the table as if Marjorie wasn't there.

"What are you going to do?"

Dietrich said nothing. He turned the switch on an overhead light and walked to a corner where large glass containers of liquid sat on shelves. Each had an object within. He grabbed two, carried one in each arm, and set them on the table.

"These are a portion of my collection," he said. "Berry Lake has provided some fine additions." He lifted a jar, and inside, a nearly round, soft-looking organ, four inches long and with a tail, floated in liquid. "Abigail Hicks contributed two fine kidneys. I gave one away as a gift. Kidneys purify toxins from the body, and Abigail was pure. Now I own the best part of her."

He set the jar on the table and lifted the other. Inside was a tapered object. "This gets people in trouble. It's a tongue. Amy Chapman's tongue, to be exact. She would have done well to keep it from flapping, but I ended that."

"I am intrigued by a person's most prominent feature and want to make it mine. Take Elizabeth Beckman, the woman whose heart I gave you as a gift. She had a very warm heart, and I thought you might benefit. Did you appreciate it? I don't think so."

He returned the two jars and brought back two more. "Sometimes an opportunity presents itself, and I never walk away." He set the bottles on the table, and Marjorie gagged at seeing an apple-sized fetus.

"This woman made the best contribution yet. It's a boy. I haven't decided on a name, but I'm thinking of George or maybe Thomas. What do you think?"

He put it down and lifted the other bottle. "This girl had the voice of an angel. Unlike you, she thought I was wonderful and gave me the best part of herself: her blooming womanhood. I hope to use her reproductive organs well."

Dietrich returned the jars to the shelf, came back, and set another bottle filled with liquid on the table, but empty. He stood with his arms folded, looking at Marjorie on the floor with her eyes stuck open and struggling to hold her head. The pieces Dietrich had taken from the human beings he had killed sickened her. *What does he want from me?*

"You're probably wondering what I want from you. I wanted you to like me at first. I invited you to the prayer group. I could tell you thought you were better than us. Everyone confessed their sins before the community of God, except you. Oh no, not you!" His voice grew louder and higher in pitch.

"Your stuck-up attitude and icy heart were your sins." Dietrich was becoming agitated, moving his arms and jabbering. "You know what the bible says, 'Pride goes before destruction and a haughty spirit before a fall.' Well, Marjorie Best, now is your destruction; you're about to fall."

He walked over, pushed her back to the floor, undid her robe, tore open her nightshirt, and screamed, "I want these breasts!" She reached up and clawed at his eyes, but he struck a hard blow to her head, and everything went black. She woke up on the table with her hands and feet bound and midsection strapped down. Naked and unable to move, she began screaming. She turned her head from side to side as she tried to loosen the plastic ties on her wrists, but they only dug deeper into her flesh.

Dietrich busily pulled instruments from the satchel and set them beside her. He wore blue surgical scrubs and held up a surgical knife with a sneer. The expression was like nothing Marjorie had seen on a person. It wasn't hatred, she saw, and it wasn't vengeance. It was a look of completion. He wanted to complete himself.

He lit his headlamp, and the light shined on her chest. "I don't usually perform my procedures while my patients are awake. They are usually dead. But I'm making an exception for you. I'm going to let you watch before I kill you."

He bent over her, and Marjorie looked. He spread the skin on the side of her left breast, ready to make an incision, when a loud crack rang out. His headlamp dropped from his head. He looked dazed, and his eyes swam in their sockets. Phoebe held a four-foot lead pipe with both hands, sending a second blow onto his head; Dietrich fell with a thud. "I think he's dead," she shouted.

"Cut me loose with those scissors," Marjorie said. Phoebe dropped the pipe, cut the plastic ties on her hands and feet, and unstrapped the restraints around her midsection. She handed her the robe, and Marjorie covered herself. She put her arm around the girl's shoulder and slid off the table.

"I thought you went for help," Marjorie said.

"I couldn't leave you here alone."

"Let's go," Marjorie said as she leaned on the girl, and they hobbled toward the stairs. It had stopped raining, and a faintly lit sky shone outside the basement window. Marjorie hoped she could get to the road and stop a car. She started up the stairs, and her leg sent bolts of pain up her side and into her back. There was movement behind her, and her heart pounded. *He's alive!*

Dietrich screamed, "You fucking bitch!" She looked over her shoulder. He used the table to climb up. Blood covered his face.

"Come on, Marjorie; we have to hurry," Phoebe said. "He's getting up."

They reached the fourth step, and Marjorie screamed when a shot rang out. She fell backward and tumbled to the floor. Phoebe looked at her with horror plastered on her face as fiery pain ripped into Marjorie's upper back.

A light lit up the room from the outside, and Phoebe shouted, "It's a car!"

Dietrich ran over and grabbed her. "You little shit, you're my ticket out of here." The girl kicked his knee, and Dietrich screamed. He slapped the child, pushed her against the floor, and tied her hands behind her back.

"You do that again, and I'll break your neck. Now let's go." Marjorie watched him take Phoebe. With her back burning from the gunshot wound, she could do nothing to help.

CHAPTER THIRTY-TWO

Maddy

The rain had stopped, and daylight broke as Maddy arrived at the old Victorian house. Tall grass surrounded the bumpy dirt road, making her feel she was in a tunnel. Reaching the end of the road, she saw the house standing in the fog against a gray open field. The Jeep's headlights shone on a white Cadillac parked on the side of the house when she reached the end of the road.

Jesus, that's Dietrich's car! She hit the brakes as a man emerged using a girl as a shield. It was Dietrich and Phoebe. He raised his arm and fired three times. Maddy dropped to the passenger seat as his first round struck the Jeep's front window, barely missing her. The second and third rounds took out the headlights.

She pushed open the driver's door, crawled out, and lay flat, ready to return fire, but Dietrich and Phoebe had disappeared into the field behind the house. Maddy followed. The sky had lightened; she saw movement at the end of the field and eased her way in its direction. When she reached the woods, she stepped inside and heard Phoebe's voice echoing among the trees. "Leave me alone," the girl shouted; Maddy followed the sound.

Reaching an open space that dropped to a stream, daylight shone, and Dietrich stood across the divide, holding Phoebe by the hair, waiting. He fired two shots; one whizzed by Maddy's head, and the other hit the tree she darted behind. She paused, glanced out, and they were gone. Continuing down the hill, she crossed the stream and ascended the other side.

Reaching the top, she looked around, saw no one, and thought she'd lost them. She spotted Dietrich and the girl walking along a ridge line. Instead of climbing, she followed from the base, keeping them in sight until they vanished.

Moving upward toward the top of the ridge, she crawled when she approached the crest, knowing she'd make an easy target if she stood. She peeked over, and Dietrich was waiting.

"Come on down, Reynolds," he said, crouching behind Phoebe with his weapon pointing at her.

"That's right," he taunted. "Let's see how good you are, Miss Big Shot Detective. I'm no Cupid; I could have taken him out in the twinkling of an eye." Maddy darted behind a tree, and a shot rang out, striking the bark near her head.

"Almost got you that time," he laughed. He was fifty yards away, and holding Phoebe tightly to his body, Maddy didn't take him out. She waited, looked, and they were gone.

Following for what felt like twenty minutes, she realized she'd lost them. *Fuck, where are they?* She stopped pursuing, sat on a fallen tree, listening for any sound that might be them, and started questioning herself.

I should have taken that shot while I had it. As she waited, thoughts of the spunky, precocious child filled her head. She recalled the girl holding her hand as she lay incapacitated on her kitchen floor after dialing 9-1-1 and saving her life. Maddy still felt Phoebe's warmth snuggling up to her back the night the girl first came to her house. Her insides were shredding at the thought of finding the child dead. She called upon her father as she had done in times of trouble. *Help me find this girl, Dad.*

The forest was alive with birdsong, but Amos Whitfield and Phoebe were gone. Maddy's instinct forced her to stay put. She listened for any sound that might be them, and finally, it came. A tree branch broke in the distance behind her. *Son-of-a-bitch, he circled back.*

Maddy moved in the direction opposite of where she had been going. She stepped into a state-maintained fire trail and remembered Amos Whitfield always had a backup plan. *He probably has a car hidden where the trail crosses a road,* she thought. *That's his destination.*

The trail extended east and west as far as she could see. Daylight was breaking in the east, and she knew it was the direction of the nearest road, so she followed the sun.

She realized if Whitfield were to arrive at his vehicle before she caught up, he'd take off and eventually kill the girl; she had to hurry. Running through calf-high grass that hid ruts and rocks might cost her a sprained ankle, and it would be over for the child if that happened. Yet she had to compensate for the gap the killer had created and ran with her eyes glued on the ground ten feet ahead, jumping over obstacles. *I need to reach her; don't let me fall.*

The trail's gradual descent made it challenging to keep her balance, and each time she stumbled, she'd slow and get her bearings before continuing.

The decline allowed her to see several hundred yards ahead, and occasionally, she glanced up, looking for movement, but couldn't see them. Sustaining a consistent, rapid pace, Maddy was glad for the hours of sprinting the hill behind her house.

She thought she saw a flash of light, possibly a car on a road, and paused. She noticed two parallel power lines stretching far into the distance. *That must be the intersection of the trail and road. He must have a car hidden there.* She didn't know how far she was from the serial killer and Phoebe, so she increased her speed.

I have to move faster. Phoebe is dead if I let them escape. Charging the rough grasses, Maddy tried to avoid the thorny bull thistles. The sun blazed, flies buzzed, and sweat dripped into her eyes. Despite running all out, Whitfield and Phoebe were still not in sight. She wondered if she had miscalculated and they had gone a different way. She climbed a twenty-foot rise where the land banked up on her right to get a better view.

She saw a redhead bobbing a hundred yards out. Looking closer, she spotted Whitfield. A car zoomed by on the road, two hundred yards away. *That's where Whitfield has a getaway car.*

Running as fast as she could through the trees on the high ground, she started closing the gap but stopped when they arrived at a car hidden in the tall grass. She was sixty yards away. Whitfield brought Phoebe to the back of the vehicle, opened the trunk, and as he put the girl inside, Maddy aimed, but the car blocked her line of fire. He raised his hand to strike the girl with the gun, and she sent a round into the ground behind him. Appearing uncertain, Whitfield glanced around, searching for the shooter, holding Phoebe in front as a shield.

Maddy ran to get a better angle; he saw her and fired three shots. One caught the fleshy part of her calf. *Shit!* she cried out in pain.

"Got you that time," he bellowed as she ran behind a tree. Her lower leg was on fire. She peeked around, and he shot again. The bullet hit the bark near her face, sending splinters into her eyes.

I have to stop him from getting Phoebe into that fucking car. She wiped her eyes clean with a handkerchief and stuffed it into her pant leg to stop the bleeding. Sweating and her lower leg burning up, she reached into her pocket for the St. Michael medal, steeling herself for the coming moment of truth. Zep's words came back to her. *He'll overplay his hand. Let him. He's most vulnerable when he thinks you're scared, and that's when you make your move.*

"Let's work something out, Whitfield," she shouted, knowing it wasn't possible to compromise with the stone-cold killer. "You let Phoebe go, and I'll come out and drop my weapon. It will take us at least an hour to walk back into town. You'll be long gone by that time." Maddy removed her jacket and tied it into a ball as she spoke.

"That's an enticing deal, Reynolds," he said. "First, throw away the gun and show yourself. Then I'll let the girl go."

Maddy's heart pounded. *It all comes down to this. Just let me have four inches; that's all I need.*

She threw the jacket on the left side of the tree, and Whitfield fired. Simultaneously, Maddy jumped out the right side, hit the ground, and aimed at a small gap between Phoebe's head and Whitfield's. She pulled the trigger; the round struck his left eyebrow, and Whitfield's head popped back. He stammered with his mouth open. Disbelief riddled his face; Phoebe dropped to the ground.

Whitfield forced his weapon up for another shot, but Maddy fired first, striking where his right arm and shoulder met; the gun fell.

Glaring at Maddy like it couldn't be happening, he reached for Phoebe. As she fired, Maddy thought of the chanting people at the stream, crying for justice. Slugs into his right and left eyes blew brains out the back of his head, and Whitfield's body lurched back, hitting the ground as his arms flopped behind him. Phoebe glanced at the bloody mess, but Maddy shouted, "Don't look at that; look at me." She hobbled to the girl, freed her hands, and hugged her.

"He shot Marjorie," Phoebe cried. "Somebody needs to help her." Maddy leaned on her, and they started gimping to the open road, then toward the Victorian house where Marjorie was. The sound of a helicopter grew louder as it circled above, finally landing on the side of the road.

Hannah Bates and two others ran towards them. Looking at Maddy's blood-soaked pant leg, Hannah said they needed to get her medical attention.

Sheriff and FBI vehicles arrived at the scene, and Maddy pointed to where the serial killer lay.

"Whitfield is over there; he's dead. Marjorie's at the address I gave you and is shot."

Hannah said they found her and had transported her to the hospital in Lake Placid. "Her husband is with her."

"I need to see Marjorie," Phoebe cried.

•   •   •

Maddy, Phoebe, and Lester sat in a waiting room at the small rural hospital. Phoebe rested her head on Lester's lap as he stroked her hair. Over two hours passed while Marjorie was in surgery, and they waited. The bullet had missed the bone on Maddy's leg, and the wound required stitches, but she could walk with crutches.

A woman dressed in blue scrubs appeared after 10:00 AM with a mask on her chest.

"I'm Dr. Carlson. I performed the surgery," she said. "It was a close one, but she will be okay. The bullet missed vital organs. She'll need to take it easy for several weeks after she comes home."

"How soon will that be?" Lester asked.

"Three or four days," Dr. Carlson said. "She's asleep now, so you should go home and rest. You'll be able to talk with her tomorrow."

"Can we look at her?" Phoebe asked.

"I think we can arrange that," the surgeon said, smiling.

Marjorie lay on her stomach with her head turned, and she appeared to be sleeping when they walked into the recovery room. Lester and Phoebe walked up close as Maddy stayed back and watched them gently stroking Marjorie's arm.

CHAPTER THIRTY-THREE

Maddy

It was a sunny September morning, and a warm breeze wafted up the mountain behind Maddy's house. Her hair blew back as she carried her coffee to the Jeep. Hurrying as she drove, she passed through the village on her way to Albany. She was going to bring Adam home, and anticipation riddled her insides. Before she started the long trek, she stopped at Lester and Marjorie's house and walked to the door. She knocked, and Lester answered.

"Come in," he said. "The girls will be down soon. They have been mighty busy this morning."

She heard Phoebe call, "Close your eyes, Lester." Lester smiled, closed his eyes, and said they were closed.

Phoebe walked down the stairs and entered the room with Marjorie behind her. The girl's beaming smile lit up the freckles on her cheeks, and the curls in her long red hair bounced as she walked into the room wearing a blue dress with pink flowers.

"Okay, you can open your eyes now, Lester."

Maddy watched as he looked at the child; she thought she saw tears gathering in his eyes. He kneeled on one knee as Phoebe ran to him. Holding her, he said, "You look stunning."

"Would you like coffee?" Marjorie asked Maddy.

"No, that's okay. I have a cup in the Jeep. I'm picking up Adam this morning and have a long drive ahead."

"But aren't you going to watch me get on the school bus, Maddy? Today's the first day."

Maddy chuckled. "I wouldn't miss it," she said.

"I think I hear it now," Marjorie said. Lester grabbed a camera while Marjorie went to the kitchen for a mermaid lunch box. Phoebe slipped her arms into a purple backpack and took the lunch box. As they started moving outside, she stopped, looked at Marjorie, and asked, "Where's Ginger?"

Marjorie unzipped a side pocket of the backpack and pulled Ginger out. "Right here," she said.

Phoebe took the soapstone rocking horse, kissed it, and put it back. They walked outside, and the bus stopped in front of the house. Phoebe looked at the bobbing heads of the kids inside with wide eyes.

"Wow!" she said. She turned to Marjorie, wrapped her arms around her waist, did the same with Lester, and smiled at Maddy. She stopped before stepping onto the bus, looked at the adults, and waved as Lester snapped a photo.

Marjorie and Lester stood next to one another, and Lester put his arm around his wife's waist as they gazed at the bus driving away. *A family is born*, Maddy thought.

·　　　·　　　·

When she was finally on her way, Maddy's mind strayed. Meandering through the winding mountain roads, she tried to grasp everything that had happened in the ten weeks since she and Adam had traveled that way together. It was as though they had entered distinct realities that summer, separated by experiences entirely inaccessible to the other. She wondered how far apart they had drifted.

The butterflies in her stomach reminded her of the day she first suspected her marriage with Jack was failing. The hollow sadness began many sorrows, ending in the greatest tragedy of her adult life—her divorce.

She tried pushing the thoughts from her head, aware she was experiencing flashbacks triggered by being away from him. She understood how people change after extended separations. It had been the longest she and Adam had been apart.

Before she reached Albany, she dialed Amber and put her phone on hands-free.

"Hi, Mom," her daughter said when she answered.

"Good morning, dear. I hope I'm not waking you."

"No, I'm just enjoying tea before I wake the girls. They are starting school again today. How are you?"

"I'm happy I can talk with my daughter without feeling angry or guilty. I'm sorry we went through all of that."

"It wasn't all you," Amber said. "Todd and I were stressed about money, and I may have taken it out on you."

"I didn't know," Maddy said.

"I didn't want you to know; I was too embarrassed."

"Do you want to talk about it?"

"No, we've been making adjustments. We dropped our membership at the country club and sold the boat; the payments were killing us. We're doing more things with the kids around our neighborhood now."

"It sounds like you two have made some excellent decisions," Maddy said.

"Yeah, I think so. I have to rush you off the phone, sorry. I hear the twins arguing. Talk soon; love you." Sighing, Maddy was relieved she and her daughter were back on an even keel. Their relationship had endured a long, stressful summer.

She grabbed the directions and followed them to the Creekside Rehabilitation Center. When she arrived, the place looked more like a community college than a medical facility, with its elegant landscaping and ponds.

She pulled under an overhang, got out, and walked inside. The tension in her stomach grew into a knot as she entered a lounge with sofas, hardwood floors, and lush oriental carpets. It resembled a hotel lobby. She asked for Adam's room at the front desk, and the woman said she'd buzz him.

"Make yourself comfortable," she said. Folding her arms, Maddy sat on a cushioned chair, bobbing her leg and thinking of how to restart the relationship with the only man she'd ever truly loved.

"Maddy," a voice called to her.

Adam stood, smiling and leaning on crutches, his head full of hair. She wanted to smile for him, but her heart sank, tears welling up as she thought of his wish to walk without a cane.

Wrapping her arms around his neck, she kissed him and looked up into his eyes, remembering how much she loved the man.

"I can't believe this day is finally here," he said. She sighed and leaned her head against his chest.

"Me too," she said.

A woman stood with Adam's belongings on a luggage cart. "The Jeep is out front," Maddy said.

She and Adam walked to the Jeep, and the woman followed. Maddy opened the back hatch, and as Adam and the woman handed her luggage items, she placed them in the back of the Jeep.

The woman waited by the cart. Adam turned to her, handed her his crutches, and said goodbye. He turned back to Maddy, smiling. "Look, Maddy, no crutches." He walked to her with his arms open, pulled her close, and they wept with joy, holding one another tightly.

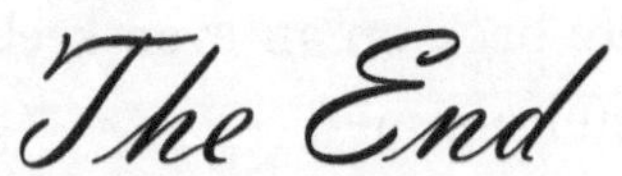

The End

ABOUT THE AUTHOR

John spent the early years of his career as a rehabilitation counselor offering a hand to people in need. Some took it, and with them, John was privileged to share their journeys. He learned of real human suffering, the tragedies, and the victories of life. But most of all, he realized we share a never-ending quest to be known. He is dedicated to making his characters known to his readers, even if just for a little while. John now writes full time, has published *Cupid, The Glades, The Ledger, Jacobi Park, Pieces,* and has plans for several other novels.

"The Glades is a spellbinding potboiler that keeps
readers holding their breath up to the very end."
-Megan Davidson, author of The Thundering

THE

GLADES

JOHN NETTI

NOTE FROM JOHN NETTI

Word-of-mouth is crucial for any author to succeed. If you enjoyed *Pieces*, please leave a review online—anywhere you are able. Even if it's just a sentence or two. It would make all the difference and would be very much appreciated.

Thanks!
John Netti

We hope you enjoyed reading this title from:

BLACK ROSE
writing™

www.blackrosewriting.com

Subscribe to our mailing list – *The Rosevine* – and receive **FREE** books, daily deals, and stay current with news about upcoming releases and our hottest authors.
Scan the QR code below to sign up.

Already a subscriber? Please accept a sincere thank you for being a fan of Black Rose Writing authors.

View other Black Rose Writing titles at www.blackrosewriting.com/books and use promo code **PRINT** to receive a **20% discount** when purchasing.